TAMING THE TWISTED 2 RECONSTRUCTING RAIN

Jodie Toohey

Wordsy Woman Press

Jodie Toohey
Wordsy Woman Press
Davenport, Iowa, 52806
www.jodietoohey.com

Book Layout © 2014 BookDesignTemplates.com

Title Page Tornado photo "in the public domain in the United States" retrieved from http://commons.wikimedia.org/wiki/File%3ATornado_of_1860_-_History_of_Iowa.jpg. Originally appearing in *History of Iowa from the Earliest Times to the Beginning of the Twentieth Century* by Benjamin F. Gue in 1903.

Taming the Twisted 2 Reconstructing Rain/ Jodie Toohey – 1st ed.
ISBN-13: 978-0692142950 (Wordsy Woman Press)
ISBN-10: 0692142959

ACKNOWLEDGEMENTS

Thank you to everyone who read the book and provided feedback, namely Mary Davidsaver, Mary Griswold, Brenda Jacobs, and LeRoy Toohey. Thank you to my wonderful editor, Misty Urban, for her above-and-beyond work. Thank you to Dustin Solomen for the cover design and formatting. Special thanks to all of the readers of *Taming the Twisted* and their encouragement to write the sequel.

Thank you to all of the curators of historical information both online and off, including, but definitely not limited to, the Clinton (Iowa) Public Library, Camanche (Iowa) Public Library, Camanche (Iowa) Historical Society, Clinton (Iowa) Historical Society, Heritage Canyon (Fulton, Illinois), Davenport (Iowa) Public Library, and Herbert Hoover Historical Museum (West Branch, Iowa).

Thank you to Midwest Writing Center (mwcqc.org) for all of the connections, information, instruction, encouragement, and support.

Thank you to my husband for supporting my dream and allowing me to be the real me. Thank you also to my children, mom, family, and friends who also may not completely understand me, but who support and love me nonetheless.

Dedicated to Lyle Ernst (1938-2016).
In addition to being a great fellow author who
was fun to be around, Lyle was an enthusiastic
beta/test reader for the first *Taming the Twisted*,
and it was probably mostly at his behest that I
rearranged my writing projects to get this sequel
finished.
Thank you, Lyle, and rest in peace.

PART ONE

CHAPTER ONE

Wednesday, June 17, 1862

For the fourth morning in a row, Alice was left to watch her twin brothers, Samuel and David, as her older sister, Abigail, left the breakfast eggs sizzling in the pan and ran to the outhouse. This time, Alice followed her. As she got closer, she could hear the barking sound that signaled violent vomiting. She waited, facing the door with her arms crossed.

Abigail emerged, her face white and drawn.

"I'm sorry. Did you need to go?" Abigail asked.

"I'm going to get the doctor."

"No!"

"Why not? You've done this all week. Something must be wrong."

"Nothing is wrong." Abigail put her hand on Alice's shoulder. "I'm fine."

"But…"

"No. I don't need the doctor. And if you tell him, you're going to be in big trouble."

"If you're fine, why do you care?"

"Just do as I tell you."

Alice puffed and stomped back to the house. She worried, but she didn't want to get in trouble with Abigail, so she lied about needing to pick up supplies for a surprise dessert at the store and went to town to ask her best friend, Lucy, her opinion, planning to next try the doctor if Lucy didn't know. Lucy had warmed to Abigail in the year and a half since Lucy's mother admitted to killing Marty Cranson, who died at the same time as but not because of the June 3, 1860, tornado, but their friendship had not been completely re-paired. Alice looked for any possible way to include Lucy in her life in an effort to keep the positive momentum moving. She loved Lucy, and she was the only real friend she'd made since moving to Camanche. As she walked toward town, she thought about those first tense days after Lucy's mother, Pamela Mackenrow, was sent to the asylum.

The early new-autumn chill had scraped Alice's cheeks. It had only been two weeks since Lucy's mother admitted to killing Marty Cranson, but the Mackenrow house already looked faded and lifeless. Lucy hadn't been to school. Alice's fist shook as she knocked on the door jamb, wondering if the scenario of rage and tears she had imagined would play out. She rubbed her fingers over her palm to try to dry the sweat that had formed on it. A burst of wind scattered a pile of crisp leaves, and she smelled a hint of fresh tea. She heard movement on the door's other side and sucked in her breath.

Mr. Mackenrow opened the door. The whites of his eyes were striped with red lines and the odor of whiskey drifted out.

He rubbed his eyes. "Alice, so nice of you to stop by."

"May I … May I speak with Lucy, please?"

Mr. Mackenrow closed the door and disappeared into the house, returning a minute later. "I'm sorry. Lucy isn't feeling well. You understand why. She's not up to visitors today."

"Alright. Shall I come by tomorrow?"

James shook his head.

"Next week after school?"

"Lucy will likely be feeling poorly for quite a while. When she goes back to school, she'll be ready for visitors."

Alice shook her head, trying to hold back the tears. "Is there anything I can do? Do you need anything from the store?"

"No, thank you. I'll tell Lucy you said hello."

"And that I miss her?"

James nodded and closed the door. The click sounded hollow in the chilly fall air.

After that, Alice waited until the last possible moment before going into school and studied the clock until it was too late for Lucy to arrive on time. Part of it was concern over her friend's wellbeing. Alice remembered what it was like after her parents had died in the tornado; she'd felt like she was in an unreal fog for weeks, her head full like when she was ill or deep into a strange dream. But part of it was curiosity; Alice had heard stories about the asylums and she wondered if Lucy had been there yet.

Even now, a year and a half later, she still didn't know if Lucy had ever gone to the asylum to visit her mother. Their rare visits seemed to be better when they'd both pretended to forget they'd ever had mothers. This made her think of her own mother, ripped away as suddenly as Lucy's, but at least Lucy's mother was alive. And her father.

There were still mornings Alice awoke, expecting him to jump out from the other side of a wall, the memory enough to take her from rubbing her sleepy eyes to fully awake. Having Marshall there was nice, but he wasn't a father.

Though he worked and eased the burden of caring for the family, farm, and home, he felt more like an older brother. Many nights, she lay awake clutching her blanket to her chin, every creak and groan or animal talk startling her away from sleep. The only cure seemed to be running through her days as hard as possible so she fell into bed too exhausted to hear anything.

The sun beat down on Alice's head, tiring her now as she reached the first row of neat houses along the Mackenrow's street. Her thoughts drifted back to Lucy and those first weeks after her world was turned upside down to more closely match Alice's.

It was a Tuesday in mid-November 1860, when Lucy returned to school. Alice had stopped watching the clock or waiting so long to go in as the weather got colder with winter on its way. She was reviewing her spelling words when she heard a commotion toward the back of the school room. She turned, but it took a moment for her to register it was Lucy. She looked so much older with her hair up in an adult twist and her hands primly folded together in front of her. But she was still Lucy and the excitement of having her best friend back at school bubbled inside. Alice ran to Lucy and threw her arms around her. Lucy hugged her back, but stiffly, and Alice could feel her bones through her thin skin.

What a different day it was compared to that day. As cold as the wind was that day, it was now warm on Alice's cheeks. It took so much time, but Lucy slowly came around. She tried again to break through the Sunday before the religious Thanksgiving observance that same year.

Alice approached Lucy after church. "Would you like to come over this afternoon to work on needlepoint?"

"No, thank you. I need to make my father dinner."

"You could come out after dinner. Or I could even help you."

"It's alright," Mr. Mackenrow said. "Go on ahead with Alice. I'm rather tired and I'm not hungry anyway, so I think I'll just relax this afternoon. I don't need a big Sunday dinner. I can find something to eat."

Lucy shrugged her shoulders. She was quiet on the walk to Alice's house.

Alice had tried to talk to her while they worked on their samplers. "Was it difficult to go back to school?" she asked.

"A little."

"If you're behind, I can help you catch up."

"I'm nearly all caught up. I worked on my studies while I was at home."

"Have you noticed the new boy, Ian?"

"Yes, I spoke to him once or twice."

"I think he likes you."

"Maybe."

Alice considered drawing Lucy out by asking her how she felt about Ian, but she seemed to be concentrating on her sampler.

"I just finished reading the best book. It was *The Marble Faun,* by Nathanial Hawthorne, about four artists in Italy. Abigail and I got so intrigued by it that we read every night until we could barely hold our eyes open. We finally finished it last night."

"Uh huh."

"I suppose once they're married, those things will be over. At least Marshall will be there, too. I don't know why Abigail gets so in a fix about the wedding. It will just be our family and Mrs. Alban – and you. You're invited if you'd like to come. Do you think you will come?"

Alice turned toward Lucy, barely rocking in her chair, concentrating on her project. The fire crackled, and Alice could feel the warming air reddening her cheeks. She continued. "Anyway, Abigail says the reading helps her to relax so she can sleep at night. I suppose after the wedding, she won't have anything to fret over." Alice turned her attention to her needlework, hoping that Lucy would take the chance to contribute to the conversation, but she didn't. "Have you read any good books lately?"

"No. Outside of the housework and homework, I haven't had any time to read."

"Perhaps you and your father could take turns reading to each other in the evenings like Abigail and me."

"Perhaps."

"I could loan you the one we just finished if you like."

"I suppose."

Alice ran upstairs to get the book from those she'd lined up on her floor beneath her window. *One day, I'll get a real bookcase*, she thought. But that wanting didn't temper her excitement at finally finding something over which she and Lucy could connect again. Alice rushed back down the stairs with the book and held it out to Lucy, who looked up, distracted.

"Oh," she said. "I'm in the middle of an important stitch."

Alice lay the book softly next to Lucy's chair and sat down in her own place. The rest of the afternoon passed in near silence.

Alice was thankful she was assured a better reception as she knocked on Lucy's door these many months later. Lucy opened it, her red hair pulled together at the back of her head.

"Alice! Is everything alright? I wasn't expecting you today."

"Yes, well, I don't know." Alice told Lucy about the sudden sickness that seemed to grip her sister like clockwork every morning.

"Maybe you should talk to Dr. Ireland."

"That's what I was thinking. I tried to get her to go see him, but she wouldn't. She said she would be fine and that she had too much to do."

"I know. Let's go ask Mrs. Alban," Lucy said.

Mrs. Alban hired Abigail on for sewing when she got busy repairing and replacing everyone's clothing after the tornado destroyed so much of people's belongings. Since then, she'd become like part of their family.

"Great idea. She always knows what to do, and she's always happy to get company."

"And maybe she has some lemonade."

The girls knocked together on Mrs. Alban's door. Alice's mouth watered, anticipating the hoped-for lemonade.

Mrs. Alban beamed as she opened the door. "Alice. Lucy. What are you doing here? Abigail isn't working today."

"We know," Alice said. "We came to see you, that is, if you're up for visitors."

"Of course. Come in. Would you girls like some lemonade? I just squeezed a fresh batch."

Lucy and Alice exchanged a knowing glance. "Yes, please," they said in unison.

Alice savored the tart liquid and felt the grains of the not-yet-dissolved sugar against the roof of her mouth as she rubbed them with her tongue. She felt the cold of the ice-cooled liquid flow down her throat.

The girls enjoyed their lemonade as Mrs. Alban chatted about the challenges of her latest sewing project. "How is everyone at home?" she finally asked, turning toward Alice. "Are those brothers of yours staying out of trouble?"

"Yes, ma'am. But…"

"What is it, dear?"

Alice took a deep breath and set her glass of lemonade by her feet. "It's Abigail. She's been getting terribly ill each morning. I've tried to get her to see the doctor, but she says she always feels better by lunch time."

Mrs. Alban grinned. "I've been waiting for this," she said wistfully.

"So you know what it is?"

"Yes, I remember it very well with my son. I was so ill every day for months, but it was all worth it in the end."

Alice looked at Lucy to see the confusion on Lucy's face that Alice could feel on her own.

Mrs. Alban said, "I do believe you are about to become an auntie, Alice."

"What?"

"It sounds to me like Abigail is in the family way. With child." She whispered the last phrase.

"Oh." Alice suddenly felt embarrassed; she knew how babies were made.

After finishing their lemonade, the girls left. Alice dropped Lucy off at her house and was almost to the edge of town before she remembered the surprise dessert she was supposed to be making. She went back to the store, got the ingredients, and tried to concentrate on the upcoming baby part of the whole business with her sister. She thought back to the day Abigail and Marshall were married on Saturday, December 15, 1860.

Snowflakes had drifted by the windows, but it was warm in the church with the candles burning. In the back room where Alice tried to put the finishing touches on Abigail's elaborate twist, frost etched the window, reminding Alice of the lace delicately sewn along the perimeter of their grandmother's handkerchief, which Abigail would carry down the aisle. It was faintly stained in one corner from where it had glued in the mud after being swept out of the house during the tornado, but folded, the stain was hidden.

Abigail's eyes darted from window to window. "Stop moving until I get the pins in place," Alice said.

She saw Abigail's jaw stiffen. "I'm sorry," Abigail said. "I just wonder…"

"Wonder what?"

"I wonder if …" Abigail clenched her fists together and dropped them into her lap. "Oh, nothing. Marshall is a good man, isn't he?"

Alice slid the last hair pin over Abigail's smooth, black hair, and then stood in front of her sister. "Of course I think Marshall is a good man. Don't you remember how I wanted him for my own husband when I was a little girl?"

Abigail's face softened. "Little girl? It was last summer."

Alice stood straight and stiff, trying to appear taller. "Well, I've grown up a lot since then." She took the mirror they had brought from home and held it in front of Abigail's face. "There, all done. What do you think?"

Abigail took the mirror and turned her head from side to side. "Wow, Alice. It looks wonderful. Thank you."

The minister's voice carried around the wall. "It's almost time. Are we ready?"

Alice looked at Abigail. "Well? Are we ready?"

Abigail nodded her head in agreement.

Alice watched Abigail walk down the aisle in their mother's wedding dress and thought Abigail looked beautiful, despite how she and Mrs. Alban had to add pieces to make the gown fit Abigail's wider waist. They'd assured Alice not to worry, that the dress could be easily taken back in when it came time for Alice to wear it, but Alice wasn't worried. Months ago, she had picked out a dress from Lucy's mother's *Godey's Lady's Book*, carefully tearing the page from the magazine so Mrs. Mackenrow wouldn't notice it was gone. She'd folded and tucked it between the pages of her diary. She was not sure that she ever wanted to be married, but if she did, she wanted to wear that dress.

It was a small ceremony. Alice stood next to Abigail while Samuel and David served as best men beside Marshall. Mrs. Alban had been invited, but she insisted she'd better stay at home to get the cake and punch ready for after the ceremony. The reverend performed the service; the twins scrunched their faces and giggled when he said Marshall could kiss the bride. After that, they all walked over to Mrs. Alban's to enjoy cake and warm punch.

That night, as Alice lay in bed and heard what should have been her mother's and father's door close behind Marshall and Abigail, she felt irritated, but knowing it was silly, she let the feeling fade away as she drifted to sleep.

Now, a year and a half later, remembering Abigail's condition, a shudder gripped her body as the thought of what else they may have been doing in her parents' bed popped into her head, but she pushed it away and concentrated on being an aunt. *I really do have a surprise dessert to make for supper now*, she thought. *I wonder how long it will take Abigail to realize that rather than*

*playing mother to her sister and brothers, she'll
be a real mother?*

CHAPTER TWO

Tuesday, July 22, 1862

The family gathered around the table for supper: roast chicken, potatoes, and mashed carrots. Abigail seemed to be eating constantly and she was getting bigger, so Alice wondered if she was finally going to tell them about the baby. Abigail had announced earlier they were all to be home on time for supper because she had something to tell them. Her cheeks were flushed, and she ate as if she hadn't just eaten a biscuit just an hour before. Alice watched her sister, waiting for an indication the news was coming.

Abigail put down her fork and opened her mouth. This is it, Alice thought, but before Abigail could get any words out, Marshall interrupted without looking up from his plate.

"I heard that today Mr. Lincoln put out a call for 300,000 men to join the fight to preserve the Union," Marshall said. He put a spoonful of potatoes in this mouth, chewed, and swallowed. "I was thinking I would volunteer."

"You can't," Abigail said.

"Why?"

"I need you here."

"It's only for a little while. You'll manage; wives all over the country are managing without their men."

"I don't even know why we're fighting the southern states. If they don't want to be a part of our country any more, we should just let them leave peacefully."

"It's not that simple, Abigail."

"Then explain it to me."

"It's the principle of it all. They are traitors revolting against their own government because they didn't get their way. We need them and they need us. We must preserve the Union. Every man who is able is going to help."

"You just can't go, that's all."

"But Abigail, I haven't heard a good reason."

With tears starting out of her eyes, Abigail choked out, her face bright red, "Because I'm … I'm having your baby." She pushed her plate toward the middle of the table, gravy splashing out onto the good tablecloth. She wiped her eyes with her napkin. "Besides, we haven't even been married for two years. I don't understand why you want to leave me already. What's wrong with me? Why does everyone I love want to leave me?"

Marshall softened and led Abigail by her elbow out of the room. Alice heard him whisper to her, "You know that it's not true that everyone you love wants to leave you. Your parents didn't choose to leave you, and I feel like I don't have a choice either. This is something I feel like I must do. And I'll be back, I promise. Mr. Lincoln says that getting more men will turn the tide. How long before the baby comes?"

"I saw Dr. Ireland today. He says about six months."

"I'll surely be back by then. You'll see, it'll be alright."

Abigail and Marshall returned to the table, her eyes blotchy and swollen. The rest of the meal passed in silence.

Nobody said anything about the baby until they were done and gathering the dishes, when Samuel asked, "What will the baby be? A sister or brother?"

Abigail dropped the dishes into the dish pan and ran upstairs. Marshall followed, undoubtedly to console her.

Alice told the boys, "No, the baby will be your niece or nephew. You're going to be uncles." They looked confused. "Do you remember Uncle Peter from Pennsylvania?"

They couldn't have, but pretended they did. Alice smiled at their vivid imaginations, but inside, her chest tightened and her stomach turned. She should have been relieved that the secret of the new baby was out and she was going to be an aunt, but instead, she grieved her world turning upside down again.

*****

Alice stood next to Abigail, resting her hand on her shoulder, her arm draped across her back. It was a typical hot mid-August day.

"It's only for a little while," she heard Abigail whisper.

"That's right. He'll be back in two weeks."

Abigail's head snapped toward Alice, her eyes glared, and she shrugged away from her. Alice sighed and let Abigail go back into the house in peace. It wouldn't do any good to argue; ever since Marshall said he was volunteering for the Union, nothing said to Abigail seemed to register anyway. She'd spent the last few weeks switching between lying in her bed staring at the wall and running to the outhouse being sick. As if the load of responsibilities had never gotten better, Alice and Marshall automatically took over the chores. Sometimes as they laughed at Samuel's and David's antics at the supper table; it felt a bit like they were a married couple, and it was nice. But then Marshall would carry a plate up to Abigail and spend the rest of the evening sitting vigil. Alice cleaned the dishes, put the boys to bed, and read one of her father's books until the sunlight disappeared into dusk, and even the lamplight wasn't enough to allow her to make out the words on the pages. She'd fall asleep imagining a faceless husband's arms wrapped around her.

Two weeks later, on Friday, Alice woke to the sounds of clanking pots below her. She dressed. Her alarm weakened when she peeked into her parents' bedroom and saw the bed empty and neatly made. Downstairs, Abigail burrowed into a lower cupboard, the curtain hung to hide the dishes behind it draped over Abigail's head.

"What are you doing?" Alice asked.

Abigail jumped, bumping her head.

"I'm sorry," Alice said, "I didn't mean …"

Abigail extracted herself and laughed as she stood. "It's alright. Did you ask me something?"

"Yes. What are you doing?"

"He's coming home today, so I was cleaning. I want everything to be perfect when Jo … Marshall gets here."

Alice considered pressing Abigail's near miss-speak, but afraid she'd drive her sister back to her room, she let it go. "I'll help," she chose instead. "What can I do? Should I sweep?"

Abigail approached Alice and placed her hands on her shoulders, a shy grin and blush spreading across her face. "There is something very important you can do for me," she said, lowering her face to stare at the floor.

"What is it?" Abigail had never had a problem with asking for her help before.

Abigail stepped back and crossed her arms in front of her chest. "I've already been to see Mrs. Alban this morning. She said it would be alright with her if you and the boys spent the night at her house …”

“But why?”

“Alice,” Abigail said, shaking her head. “I haven’t seen my husband for two weeks. We need some time alone together.”

“Oh.” Now it was Alice’s turn to redden. “Samuel and David have been marking the days until Marshall comes …”

“I know. It’s only for tonight. You and the boys can come back tomorrow morning, as soon as the sun rises if you like.”

Alice packed a bag of things they’d need for a night away from home, and as soon as she could get them ready, she took the twins to Mrs. Alban’s, leaving Abigail to her cleaning. They enjoyed their time at Mrs. Alban’s, and the hours flew by with lemonade, sweets, and games, not slowing until Mrs. Alban slumped in her chair, snoring as popcorn tipped out of her bowl onto the floor. They giggled as they picked up the mess, covered Mrs. Alban with a blanket, and crept in to crowd themselves into what used to be

Mrs. Alban's son's bed to sleep. Alice was still staring at the ceiling when she heard Mrs. Alban shuffle to her own bedroom next door.

She wondered about Abigail and if she fully realized that Marshall would be leaving again in less than two days, and this time it would be for much longer than two weeks. She began to dread the work she knew was coming as Abigail retreated into herself. She fell asleep as the dark began to lighten to blue, imagining leaning into a strong shoulder belonging to someone who could take her away and take care of her for a change.

They enjoyed the weekend; Sunday arrived too soon. Dark clouds approached from the west and faint thunder rumbled. It was terrible timing as Marshall prepared to join the Iowa 20th Infantry on its way to Davenport. The family drove the buckboard to town, loaded in the back with the children and Marshall's pack of clothes, paper, stamps, mess kit, tent muslin, canteen, and other necessities. Marshall drove until they got to the meeting place. He handed Abigail the reins and she slid over on the seat. Abigail looked straight ahead as Marshall reached over the buckboard's side and grabbed his bags. He stepped away, Abigail clicked the reins, and they drove to park the horses at the designated spot down the block.

It pained Alice to see her sister so sad, crying as Marshall hugged her goodbye and said, "I'll be back before you'll even miss me."

He hugged Alice, who barely held in her tears, and shook Samuel's and David's hands. Mrs. Alban was also there; she said not to worry, that she'd take good care of his family. Alice still didn't quite understand why he was going when it obviously hurt him so much, but she thought maybe she'd understand when she got older.

The drummers tapped on their drums and the buglers played as they marched south out of town toward Davenport and preparations to head to the front lines.

The next morning, Alice knocked softly on Abigail's door before entering the room. It was dark with the shades pulled. "Abigail, supper's ready."

"I'm not hungry."

"But the baby. You have to eat."

"I'll get something later. I just feel so weak and tired all of the time from the baby."

"Are you sure it's just the baby?"

"Yes. Please let me rest."

Alice pulled the door shut and joined her brothers for supper.

"Abigail's not coming," Samuel said.

"No, she said she'd eat later and to get started without her."

On this night, Alice felt sorry for Abigail. As she ate, she thought about how hard it must be to have so many responsibilities, with a baby on the way and no husband around. But Alice also became angry with her, thinking about the responsibilities that had fallen on her all day. Then Alice thought about how she'd feel if the husband she just married and got in the family way with decided to leave her all alone, and she'd feel sorry for her sister again. At least Abigail was married; she'd always wanted that.

CHAPTER THREE

Friday, September 12, 1862

Lucy sat on the school steps eating her lunch. Alice sat down next to her. She unwrapped her ham pieces, broke off a piece of biscuit, and popped them together into her mouth.

"It's starting to look like fall," she said. "The tree leaves are starting to change color. I just love how beautiful it is in the fall."

Lucy's eyes flared toward Alice.

"Oh, that's right. I'm sorry."

The girls went back to eating quietly.

"I'm free after school for a little while. I was thinking we could go for a walk," Alice said.

"I can't. I need to fold the laundry I hung this morning and get supper started for Father."

"I could help you. I have plenty of experience."

"If you like," Lucy said, tucking her lunch wrappings into her pail. "I need to go," she said, walking toward the outhouse.

After school, Alice grabbed her things and walked out the door, expecting Lucy to be waiting for her, but she wasn't there. Alice looked up and saw her halfway across the school yard, heading toward her house.

"Lucy, wait," she called, running to catch up with her. "I was coming with you, remember?"

"Oh, yes. Sorry. I forgot," Lucy said.

"What should we do first? Fold the clothes or start supper?"

"I'm making beef stew, so it would probably be best to get that started first."

"Great. I can help you chop vegetables."

"Alright."

Alice followed Lucy down to the cellar where Lucy silently handed the potatoes and carrots to her. All Alice could hear were the sounds of their knives hitting the cutting boards as they sliced through potatoes, carrots, onion, and beef. They slid the ingredients off the boards with the backs of their knives and they splashed into the broth Lucy had already seasoned. Alice placed their cutting board and knives in the wash tub while Lucy tested the broth and added more seasonings. When she was done, Lucy went outside to the clothes line without saying a word to Alice.

What is the matter with her? Alice thought. *I've been nothing but nice and helpful to her, and she just keeps getting colder and colder.* Alice went outside and took a place beside Lucy. She took a pair of James' jeans off the line and shook them before folding them.

"It sure is cold out here," she said.

Lucy looked at her sideways, the sun sparkling through her strands of red hair.

"Not the weather," Alice said. "I mean the way you're treating me." Alice laughed, but Lucy gave no indication of understanding the attempt at a joke. "Are you angry with me?"

Lucy shrugged.

"What have I done?"

"It wasn't what you did."

"Then what is it? Tell me."

Lucy turned, and the wind caught her hair, blowing it so it looked like flames were shooting out of her head. "It's your sister. If it wasn't for her, my mother would be here, and I wouldn't be stuck with all this housework. You keep coming around, acting like I should be able to play and do things like we used to, but because of your sister, I can't."

"I'm sorry that your mother killed Marty Cranson. My sister didn't make her do it; she just convinced your mother to tell the truth. I have a lot of work to do at home, too, you know. Both my parents died, if you remember. And Abigail's husband is off doing his patriotic duty. The way

I see it, you're better off. You only have your father to care for while I have two young boys and another baby on the way. And your mother is still alive."

Tears gathered in the corners of Lucy's green eyes. "Go away," she said. "My father didn't enlist because he didn't want to leave me all alone."

"Lucy, I didn't mean …"

"I know what they say about him. I hear them whisper as I walk by." Lucy's eyes flared in anger again. "But thanks to your family, my father is unable to serve his country."

"You blame me for that, too?"

"Just go," Lucy said. "Leave me alone."

Alice wept all the way home. She'd hated hurting Lucy, but what she'd said was true. She'd thought life would take on some sort of normalcy when Abigail and Marshall were married, and it did for a while. But, oh, how things change. Now her days were filled with taking care of children and the house, and in a few short months, all of it would increase when the baby came. Alice watched a flock of geese fly overhead, their V-formation pointing south. *How I wish I could go with them*, she thought.

*****

"The end." Alice read the last of a serial of a mystery story in the weekly newspaper. "Wow. Can you imagine? I don't know if I could ever kill anyone."

"The only real experience I have with it, of course, is with Pamela. It seems that rarely do we hear that the person who murdered someone was purely evil. They usually seem to be mentally off or mad in some way. Like Pamela. Marty Cranson did a terrible thing to her, and it made her mind sick. Pamela was never nice to me, but I don't think she is evil." Abigail rubbed her hands over her middle, which was starting to protrude.

"No," Alice said. "I was completely shocked to hear she'd confessed to killing Marty. I'd never known her to be violent. She wouldn't even swat a fly in her house, but would go to great pains to swish it outside."

The girls were silent for a long moment, watching the clouds drift in front of the stars.

Finally, Abigail broke the silence. "Sometimes I worry if I may be mad." She stared at her belly as if she could see through it to the baby growing inside.

Alice looked at her, confused.

"Not enough to kill, mind you. But I see all the ladies in town rushing to the post office every day, hoping for a letter from their husbands or beaus on the front lines. But it isn't my husband I'm looking to receive a letter from. It's Joseph."

Alice unfolded her legs and stomped her feet on the step below. "That coward. How could you even think kindly of him at all after what he did?"

"I don't know. I just keep wondering why he left and didn't say goodbye like he said he would. I wonder if his parents were actually ill, or if he decided he didn't love me anymore, so he just made it up to get away from me. He had to have heard about the tornado. Why did he never ask about my health? Did he care that little for me?"

Alice tried to think of an explanation. "I think there isn't any way to know, Abigail. Remember how Mother and Father always used to tell us when we fell and skinned our knee or if someone hurt our feelings with something they said, or if something didn't turn out the way we'd hoped, that it was God's plan? That there was a good reason things happened the way they did. We just don't know what that reason is."

"I remember."

"Maybe that's what happened here. God must have had a reason. Maybe it's so you and Marshall could find each other. So maybe you can have a family with him."

"Perhaps." Abigail got up, walked a few feet from the house, and looked up at the sky. "I find myself thinking of Joseph at night when I'm trying to fall asleep. Is he even under the same sky as me anymore? I wonder what it would be like if he came back." She swept her arm across her body like she were showing off the porch.

"What if he showed up right here, right now on this porch? He started to build this porch. It's all so strange. I don't know what I'd really do if he came back. I've gone through every scenario in my mind. In some of them, I'm overjoyed and filled with a rush of love. Other times, I'm angry and I push him away. What do you think that means?"

"Perhaps it means you are as afraid of seeing him again as you are of never seeing him again."

"It's possible."

"What about Marshall?"

"I love Marshall, of course. But the feelings I had for Joseph are still here. I still feel them the same as I did those years ago. I love Marshall. But it's not the same." Abigail sighed as she sat back down next to Alice. "When the ladies in town get a letter from their men, they are so happy. They clutch the letters to their bosoms with tears streaming down their cheeks. I feel so guilty because I feel a bit disappointed the letter is from Marshall instead of Joseph. As I read, it's like I'm reading the newspaper. Maybe I'm a terrible person."

"No, that's not it." Alice patted her sister's back and smiled at her.

Abigail half-smiled back. "Are you certain?"

"Yes. It's a hard time. People react to things differently. It'll be all right. You'll see."

"I hope so." Abigail yawned. "I'm tired. I think I'll go to bed before I feel wide awake again." She stood up and stretched. "Are you coming?"

"I think I'll sit out here a little longer," Alice said. "I'm not that tired yet."

"Make sure you lock up when you come in."

"I will."

Alice thought about what her sister had said. If Abigail were mad, then she was likely in just as sad a shape. Since Lucy stopped speaking to her, some of the other girls from school had started to notice and they'd tried to be nice to her. Alice was polite, but she refused their invitations. She'd lost her parents and Lucy. And then Marshall, whom she'd been fond of since they'd found him injured in the field the morning after the tornado. When she thought of sharing secrets with these girls, she thought about how she'd feel if she lost them, and she couldn't bear to face that pain again. Even with her brothers, she had always been an affectionate sibling, kissing, hugging, and cuddling them. But now she tried to keep her interactions with them more distanced. She took care of them, but did her best not to make them too important in her life. *If something is your whole life, it only hurts that much more when you lose it*, she thought. She wondered if that might be why Abigail focused on missing Joseph instead of her own husband. Maybe since she'd already lost Joseph, it was easier to dwell on that rather than thinking of what she'd do if she lost Marshall, too.

CHAPTER FOUR

Tuesday, January 20, 1863

Alice stood and turned to take her dishes to be washed. She heard the sound of splashing and whipped around, expecting to see one of her brothers' sheepish faces as their milk covered the floor. But instead she saw the look of shock on Abigail's face as she stood in a wet spot growing on the wooden planks.

"What happened?" Alice asked.

"I think the baby's coming," Abigail said, suddenly clutching her abdomen and doubling over.

"Let's get you upstairs and then I'll go get Mrs. Alban."

Abigail nodded her head in agreement. She leaned on Alice as they slowly climbed the stairs. They were almost to the top when Abigail doubled over in another stab of pain and sank to the ground. Alice held her to keep her from falling, and her strength had almost given out when the pain passed. She took her sister as quickly as she could to her bed. She pulled her wet shoes off and wiped her hands on her skirt. "I'll be right back. I'll take the buckboard to Mrs. Alban's."

Abigail's eyes were frantic. "No, you can't leave me." She gripped the sheet along her sides in white-knuckled fists. "Send the boys," she gasped.

"But they're only five. What if they get lost?"

Abigail shook her head on her pillow, and sweat began to trickle down the side of her forehead. "They're big boys. They've been there dozens of times. They know the way. And they're fast. They'll be there and back with Mrs. Alban by the time you get the team hitched." Abigail held her breath and scrunched up her face. It reddened like a ripe apple.

"Breathe."

Abigail's breath rushed out of her mouth like a storm. She said, "Go down and tell the boys what to do." She breathed in. "Tell them to be fast." She took a deep breath in again. "Then bring up a bowl of cool water and a cloth."

Alice did what she was told. Samuel and David streaked down the road, their heads high, proud at being given such an important task.

It seemed like hours had passed, but according to the clock hands, it had only been a few minutes when Mrs. Alban came rushing up the stairs.

Alice stayed by Abigail's head while Mrs. Alban worked to help get the baby out. She fought the urge to run away like she did when the calves were born. It took hours. Mrs. Alban said the baby's face was facing toward Abigail's back, which was an unusual position. It made it difficult for Abigail to push it out. Alice started to worry. *It's taking too long,* she thought, knowing she actually had no facts upon which to base that assumption. When it was time to push, Alice leaned into Abigail's back while at the same time pulling Abigail's bent left leg toward her.

"Almost there!" Mrs. Alban said. "The head is out."

Alice peeked between Abigail's legs. She saw a mass of black hair. She felt faint and quickly turned her attention back to Abigail's head.

"Just one or two more pushes and the baby will be here," Mrs. Alban said.

Just when Alice thought neither she nor her sister could hang on any longer, she heard Mrs. Alban say, "It's a girl!"

She watched Mrs. Alban slap her new niece's bottom. In horror, she leapt up. "What are you doing? She was just born. What could she have done?"

The baby started to cry. Mrs. Alban wrapped her in a towel, unable to control her laughter. Abigail, too, gasped with laughter, her disheveled hair plastered to her head and pillow.

"What's so funny? She just spanked a brand-new baby." The anger bubbled.

Abigail grabbed her hand. "No, no. That's what you do when babies are born. It gets them to start breathing."

Alice lowered her eyes. "Oh," she said, embarrassed. She had a lot to learn.

Mrs. Alban stayed for a full two days after Josie was born, showing Abigail how to nurse and Abigail and Alice how to bathe her. Alice examined her new niece's foot, pink and wrinkly, and wondered if she'd ever want to have a baby. She had thought she did, until she saw Josie being born. She'd seen it herself but still couldn't figure out how something Josie's size came out of you "down there." She'd never seen the calves being born and assumed they had just grown that fast since coming out.

Abigail tore, so she walked slowly. She hugged Mrs. Alban. The old woman catapulted herself into the carriage, thanking Samuel and David for taking such good care of her horse. Alice watched from the doorway, holding her swaddled niece close to her chest, protecting her from the wind, the flat brown grass surely bound to reunite with the white that should have come calling weeks ago. Sure enough, the first flakes began swirling by the window as soon as Abigail sat in the rocking chair and Alice put Josie in her arms to feed. They watched the clock and the increasing snow, not saying anything until Alice interrupted the silence.

"It's been long enough." She got up, opened the front door, and looked out. "The snow's barely covered the ground, and I can still see a ways down the road. She should be there by now."

Not looking up from Josie's face nestled into her breast, Abigail said, "Good. I was getting worried a blizzard was working up."

"Me, too."

A blizzard *was* coming, but it built slowly. The snow left a few inches on the ground, so Alice sent the boys out to play in it while she cleaned and Abigail and the baby napped. She became entranced in her sweeping and didn't notice when the boys' squeals of laughter as they sledded down the hill behind the house turned to rattling glass and wind battering the siding. She looked up to see nothing but white. She dropped her broom, wrapped her coat around her shoulders, and rushed outside.

"Boys! It's time to come in." She tried to stay calm, until they didn't answer her. She walked toward the hill. "Samuel! David!" A full panic was about to overtake her when the boys appeared out of the white, snow covering their coats and hats. Alice pulled them toward her. "Why didn't you come in when it started snowing like that?"

"We did," Samuel said.

"We were halfway down the hill, then we fell, so we had to find the sled before coming in." David stepped to the side, showing the sled he pulled behind him with a rope.

"We'd better get inside," Alice said.

"We'll put the sled away," Samuel said, heading toward the barn.

Alice grabbed the rope. "No, we'll just leave it on the porch. You can put it away when the storm's over."

The blizzard stayed for three days, drifting in still waves, some spots showing the winter grass, and some drifts toppling over like waves in mid break. Josie was still new enough to the twins that they stayed calm and quiet, looking at books and playing in their room. Neither Abigail nor Alice told them how soundly Josie slept. Once the cleaning was finished, Alice spent most her time holding her niece in her arms, falling in love. She changed her, cleaned her bottom, and listened to her breathe, only giving her up so Abigail could feed her, she could make meals, or when she needed to sleep in her own bed.

It took five days, but the sun finally reappeared from behind thick clouds and the wind calmed. Alice and the boys left Abigail and Josie alone while they trudged through snow drifts to the barn, pushing the abandoned sled ahead of them to help clear a path. They used their hands to scoop the snow away from the barn door and pulled it open. They stepped into the dark and waited for their eyes to adjust.

Alice had trudged by herself to the barn each day to service the horses and milk the cow. Even if she'd thought of it, she wouldn't have been able to carry a shovel and carry the milk pail so it didn't slosh out and freeze in the snow. By the time she'd got back to the house, she was too exhausted and cold to think about going back.

"Over there!" David said, pointing to two shovels leaning against the wall, snow gathered around the blade where it had blown through the cracks. He ran to them, grabbing their neck handles one in each hand. Alice took one.

"This time, why don't we leave them closer to the house?" She pretended to be deep in thought.

The boys laughed and nodded their heads in agreement.

For the rest of the morning, they worked to clean a wider path between the house and barn and create a path to the road where sleigh ruts already flattened the drifts as neighbors went by on their way to town. They didn't own a sleigh; Abigail had sold it right after the tornado, in a panic they wouldn't have enough money to buy provisions and fix the house, not thinking about the snow that would return in four or five months. By the time she thought to repurchase one, the prices had gone up, so they made do without. They would have to wait until the road was packed down enough to walk or melted away in the sun to accommodate wagon wheels. They weren't worried, though. Each neighbor who passed stopped to ask if they needed anything, and even when they said, "No, thank you," they were almost always neighborly and brought them back something anyway.

Samuel and David ran through the cutaway drifts, the sidewalls reaching to their waists, howling like they were in tunnels. Alice watched them, shaking her head and laughing.

"I think our work is finished," she said. "I'm going in. You coming?"

"Can't we stay and play?" David asked.

"Alright. But I thought I'd make some cocoa. Are you certain?" They shook their heads in unison. "Come in as soon as you get cold. I'll keep the cocoa warm for you."

Alice went around the house to the back door so she could lean the shovels in a more convenient spot, and so she could hang her wet coat, hat, scarf, and mittens where they wouldn't drip through the house. It was quiet, so she was careful not to wake Abigail or the baby if they were sleeping. A hint of resentment washed over her about the fact that Abigail hadn't fixed them any dinner, but then she thought of Josie and it dissipated. Alice tiptoed toward the sitting room. She was about to peek around the door when she heard Abigail whispering.

"Your daddy is going to be so proud of you." Alice leaned her head toward the wall and smiled. Abigail continued whispering. "You're named after him, you know?"

Alice snapped upright. She jumped into the doorway, her skirt swishing with the sudden movement. Abigail jumped, too.

Alice asked, "What did you say?"

"When? … What do you mean?"

"Just now. You whispered to Josie she was named after her father."

"No, I didn't. I said she was named after my mother. You must've heard wrong. Marshall is nothing like Josephine or Josie." Alice noticed Abigail's laugh seemed less than genuine, but she let the matter drop anyway.

"May I hold her for a while?"

"Certainly."

Alice scooped her niece from her sister's arms. They traded places and Alice settled into the rocking chair. "Oh, I forgot. I told the boys I'd make cocoa. And it's almost dinner time." She could be sneaky, too. "Would you mind?"

Abigail put her hands on her lower hips, bending back, her still-swollen stomach protruding and her elbows pointing outward. Her face was flushed. "I suppose it would be nice to use my *hands* to provide nourishment for someone for a change."

As she rocked Josie, Alice closed her eyes. *I think I'll marry a rich man, so I can have a housemaid and I can just rock my baby all day.*

By Friday, the sun had broken out and the temperature climbed until the melting snow began to form long icicles in the night. Samuel and David were unusually excited when Alice told them they would be going to church in the morning. They had already grown tired of playing in the snow around the house.

*****

Alice woke to Josie's screaming below. The dark had just begun to secede to predawn. Alarmed, she put on her robe and rushed downstairs to see what was wrong with her niece. Abigail was in the rocking chair, trying to hold Josie to her breast as she squirmed and howled.

"What's the matter?" Alice asked.

Abigail's eyes were red. "I don't know. She woke up at almost one. She ate, but every time I went to lay her down, she'd start crying. And now she just started screaming. She won't eat and her bottom is clean."

Alice put her hand on her niece's stomach. Josie flinched as Alice touched what felt like a balloon.

"Look at her tummy," Alice said, pushing the blanket away and pulling up the baby's gown. "I think she has a tummy ache."

Alice picked Josie up, resting the baby's head on her shoulder. She patted her back as she walked around the room, bouncing her up and down. At first, she cried harder, and Alice was about to tell Abigail to get the doctor, but then Josie released a loud belch. Alice stretched her neck and looked at Josie out of the corner of her eye; the baby had fallen fast into an exhausted sleep.

Alice turned toward Abigail. "I think she's ..."

But Abigail was asleep herself, slumped in the rocking chair. Alice used her foot to pull Abigail's leg out from under her; she slid, and the chair snapped back as she steadied herself.

"Alice!"

"Shhh. She's sleeping now. Go to bed. There's only a few hours until church."

"I can't go to church today. I'm too tired."

"We have to. We promised Samuel and David. Plus, it's Josie's baptism. Go to bed. I'll get everything ready and let you sleep as long as possible. You can go back to sleep as soon as we get back home."

Abigail shook her head and dragged herself upstairs. Alice carefully leaned into the rocking chair, gradually slowing the bouncing motion so Josie wouldn't notice. She stopped and held her breath. Josie didn't even twitch. She sat still for a few minutes to make sure she was asleep, then she laid her in the bassinet. She stretched out on the hard floor next to Josie, covered only by a thin rug, intending only to rest a minute. But the rising sun shone bright on her eyelids, waking her an hour later.

She looked at the clock: 8:13. She peeked at Josie, who hadn't moved; Alice gently rested her palm on the baby to feel her chest softly rise and fall. She started the oatmeal and went up-stairs to wake the boys, but they were already up, playing quietly. Since Josie had been born, they'd become adept at quiet.

"Time to get dressed," Alice said.

"Are we still going to church?" David asked. They'd also gotten accustomed to plans changing.

"Yes. I promised, didn't I?" They jumped into action, throwing their socks at each other. Alice laughed. "Come down as soon as you're dressed. I'm making oatmeal."

"Oatmeal," Samuel said, screwing up his face.

"Yes, oatmeal. It's all we have time for. It'll be good. I'll put brown sugar on it," she said, singing the last sentence.

The boys' smiles widened.

Alice stirred the oatmeal, which was just starting to stick to the bottom of the pan. She re-moved it from the heat and scooped it into the boys' bowls to cool before she got herself dressed. When she came back, she saw Samuel with a heaping spoon of brown sugar, ready to add it to the mound already sitting atop his oatmeal.

"Samuel! What are you doing?"

"You said we could have brown sugar."

"Not that much!"

Samuel quickly dumped the sugar onto his bowl and dropped the spoon; it clanked on the table.

"Give me that," Alice said. She scooped half of the brown sugar from Samuel's bowl and dropped it in David's. "There. That's more than either of you should eat."

She was about to drop some oatmeal in her own bowl when David said, "I'm thirsty." So she took as big of a bite as she could directly off the serving spoon and dropped it back in the pan. Hot! She made a ring with her lips and sucked in to cool the food. Her eyes watered. She held up her index finger at the boys and looked in the icebox. She swallowed the oatmeal; her tongue tingled.

"I haven't milked today, but there's a little left from yesterday you can share." She split it as evenly as she could between their two tin cups. She woke Abigail before going out to milk the cow, who she knew would be miserable if she waited until after church, her stomach growling the entire way.

Her frustration and resentment grew with each pull of the cow's nipples. The milk frothed in the bucket. And then she started to cry. The overwhelm ballooned inside until it seemed to push itself out her body through her tears and saliva pouring into her mouth. She tried to hold it back. To be cheerful. She tried to console herself. *We're going to church. It's Josie's baptism day.* But it didn't work. She leaned her forehead against Bessie's ribs and sobbed. She let it all wash over her and through her.

She missed her mother, but she missed her father even more. He was their foundation, their strength. The only person who could say every-thing was going to be alright and she would believe it. It wasn't fair. The boys were still too young to be of much help, Marshall was gone to war, and Abigail had become so weak, she was essentially useless much of the time. It all fell on her. As her body calmed, she thought about es-caping. But then she remembered the snow and cold. She breathed in deeply, wiped her eyes, and finished the milking.

CHAPTER FIVE

Tuesday, April 28, 1863

Another exhausting day. They were all starting to feel the same, running together like the creeks that emptied into the river. The lengthening days just seemed to create more hours for Alice to work. She fell into bed hours after the sun had set after finally getting time to clean the day's dirty dishes, not bothering to brush her hair. She awoke to faint cries that became louder and louder. Josie. She went downstairs to find her niece alone in her bassinet, clearly ready for her breakfast.

"Abigail," she called throughout the house, trying not to wake her brothers, bouncing Josie in her arms, attempting to calm her. She stepped out the back door and looked toward the outhouse, but the door swung back and forth in the strong spring breeze, banging against the hinge. She found Abigail in her bedroom, fast asleep on top of the bed covers. "Abigail!"

Her sister popped up. "What?" she asked, rubbing her eyes.

"It's Josie. She needs you."

"I'm so tired." Abigail looked at her bed, smoothing the quilt with her palm. "I came up to change and must've fell asleep."

Alice held her fussing niece out to Abigail, who blocked her with her hand. She started to whimper. "Alice, I'm so tired. Can't you please help me this once?"

Though she tried to keep it down so as not to upset Josie any further, she couldn't help but let her anger bubble up. "This once? I love Josie, but 'just this once' has happened constantly since she was born. Besides, I can't help with *this*. She's hungry." She pushed Josie into her sister's arms. "Only *you* can fix that." She stomped out, slamming the door behind her.

She cringed, but it was too late. David appeared in his doorway. "Is breakfast ready?"

Alice glared at him and locked herself in her bedroom.

I'm sick of this, she thought, brushing the tangles out of her hair. *I've had it. She is supposed to be the mother, but I'm the one who ends up doing everything around here. Cooking. Cleaning. Poopy butts. And soon the planting and gardening. No more.* She brushed her hair away from her face, gathering it at the crown of her head before twisting it into a bun and securing it with pins. She laced up her shoes, threw a sweater over her shoulders, and stomped out of the house while her brothers stared at her, dumbfounded.

When she got to the road, she broke into a run, screaming. She didn't get far before her ankle twisted, forcing her to slow to a walk and her frustration to release with her tears. When she got to town, she hung her head to avoid looking anyone in the eye and went around the business area through a quieter neighborhood. When she reached the river bank, she sank to the ground, folding her legs. *What am I going to do?* She left in such a hurry, she didn't think to take any money. *I should've taken the buckboard and horses.* Her feet already hurt from pounding on the ground during her short run. She cried until she was empty, and then she stared into the river, watching the water flow past. She wished she could be on a raft and float away with it. The sun climbed and she took her shawl off her shoulders, balling it in her lap. She softened as she thought of Samuel, David, and Josie. *Who'll take care of them? Maybe if I'm not there, Abigail will be forced to do it.*

She got up, smoothing her hair and hoping her reddened eyes had returned to normal. She still wasn't sure if she would go back home as she walked to the post office. There was a letter from Marshall. It was addressed to the Sinkeys, so she felt justified in reading it first.

My dearest Abigail, Alice, Samuel, David, and my newest blessing, Josephine,

I was so happy to receive your letter relaying the news of my baby girl. Please tell her that her daddy loves her and can't wait to meet her.

I'm enclosing several pages I wrote on the march here, the first chance I've had to put them in the post.

We are in Benton Barracks, in a suburb of St. Louis, about three miles from where we landed the steamer we boarded in Keokuk. You should have seen the reception we got. At every point, there were people waving flags from windows on both sides of the street along with other demonstrations of their welcoming us.

At night, I try to imagine what was like here when this place was used for the county fair. Now, many of the buildings are primarily used as hospitals. The company will be here for a while and then will head south. I will write and send more letters when I can.

Always, my love,

Marshall (Daddy)

Alice folded the letter and tucked it into her skirt pocket. She looked down the road that went out of town toward Davenport and thought of following it. But then Abigail would again be abandoned by someone she loved, or at least she would think she was. That alone didn't bother Alice as much as the worry of how much more worse off the boys and Josie would be if Abigail sank deeper into herself. Plus, Samuel and David had been asking daily if Marshall had written them a letter. So she turned toward home. *I'll find another way.*

*****

Alice pulled on the straps tethering the horses to the buckboard. They were as secure as she could make them. She poked her head in the front door. "Boys! Hurry or we're going to be late."

Abigail glared at her from where she sat nursing Josie, both of them half asleep.

"Sorry," Alice whispered. She had gotten into the habit of giving Samuel and David a ride to school on Mondays so she could bring their provisions for the week back in the wagon, saving a trip. That routine would change in a few weeks when school was out for the summer. She had planned to return to school herself to finish when the war was over and Marshall returned home, but lately she wasn't sure if she would; she already knew everything she needed to be swept away and serve as wife and mother.

So much for washing on Mondays, ironing on Tuesdays, and baking on Wednesdays that her mother had sang to her about when she was a little girl. With an older sister lost in her own world a good deal of the time and two young boys, an infant, house, and farm to care for, the chores got done whenever she found time to do them, and when Abigail was coherent enough to help. Alice was anxious for school to be finished for the year so the twins could help more on the farm.

Samuel and David rushed down the stairs, pushing each other out of the way in a race.

"Stop it!" Alice said. "You'll wake Josie. Besides, we'll be more than late to school if you two hurt each other. Come on!" She held the door open for them and they jumped on the buckboard's front seat. She took the horses' reins and thrust herself up, squishing the twins together. "Make room for me!" They giggled and hugged each other like they were trying not to fall off.

Alice dropped the boys at school just as the last students were trickling into the building. The boys rushed toward their friends, playfully shoving each other as they went. *If it wasn't for the children, life would be so dull*, she thought.

She rode to the store and secured the horses to a hitching post where they could stretch their necks to the watering troughs to get a drink. Once her eyes adjusted to the inside darkness in contrast with the bright May sun, she saw a familiar glint of red toward the back. Her heart beat a little faster. She hadn't seen Lucy in months. She had intended to call on her several times, but never got around to it.

"Lucy!" She approached with arms outstretched, ready to hug her best friend, but the look on Lucy's face stopped her, and her arms fell back to her sides.

Lucy's eyes were cold and had dark circles under them. "Alice," she said.

"You're not in school today, either?"

Lucy looked around. "No. I'm not in school most days lately."

"Oh. I'm sorry."

"No need. I'm lucky enough to get to read a few pages in my study books between the end of my afternoon chores and before starting supper for Father."

Lucy's tone irritated Alice. "That's nice. The only time I have to read is in the evenings after putting all the children to bed, and by that time, I'm so exhausted I can't hold my eyes open."

Silence was Lucy's response. She turned back toward the shelf, looking high and low for some unknown item.

Alice softened. "How is your father?"

Lucy turned back toward her, crossing her arms in front of her chest. "He works, he eats, and then he sits in a chair and drinks whiskey before starting all over again."

Alice lowered her eyes to the floor, not knowing what to say. It was obvious Lucy still blamed Abigail for her situation and was still taking it out on Alice. Alice stiffened her spine, cleared her throat, and said the first thing that popped into her mind, something she'd heard said over and over since the war began. "Our boys should take care of those gray backs soon, and then everything can get back to normal."

The words caught in Alice's throat as soon as she said them. Lucy's eyes peered at her so sharply, she wondered if knives would fly out of them into her heart.

Lucy clenched her fists and she shook, but she found some words. "Perhaps for you," she said through clenched teeth, "but this silly war has no consequence on my mother being locked up because of something your sister got her to *say* she did."

It didn't occur to Alice until she was half-way home that Lucy emphasized "say" in her last biting remark before dropping her items and stomping out of the store. *I wonder what she meant by that. Is Pamela trying to convince Lucy she didn't kill Marty Cranson?*

As Alice put her purchases away after returning home, she noticed it seemed unusually quiet but didn't think about it any more than that. She backed the buckboard into the barn, unhooked the horses, led them to their stalls, and fed and watered them. Back in the house, she held her hands on her hips and examined the area. *It's still pretty clean. I guess this week is washing on Monday after all.*

She went upstairs to gather the laundry. *They must be sleeping*, she thought. She gathered the boys' things from the pile where they'd left them on the floor into her basket along with her own. She pushed open the door to Abigail's room as quietly as she could to not wake her or Josie. She collected their clothes and was just about to grab the container of soiled diapers when she noticed Josie wasn't in her bassinet. She looked at the bed. Abigail lay sprawled on her back, but no Josie. Alice looked around downstairs and didn't see her niece anywhere. Panic began to build. *What has she done?*

She shook Abigail. "Wake up! Where's Josie?"

Abigail sat up, groggy. "What are you talking about? She was right here." She looked around the bed, but Josie wasn't there. She stiffened to a sitting position. As she did, they noticed a lump under Abigail's skirt. It wasn't moving.

"What did you do?" Alice asked, rushing to the bedside.

"I just sat down with her. I was going to change her, but I felt so tired that we lay down. I must've fallen asleep."

Alice reached out her hand but hesitated before lifting Abigail's skirt, afraid of what she would see. She was so still. *Like Mother and ... No!* She picked up Abigail's skirt with her thumb and index finger and threw it toward her sister. She peered more closely. Josie's cheeks were red. Her head was turned to the side, and she was pressed into the mattress like she was in a straw tick cocoon. Alice had almost got her palm to Josie's chest to check for breathing when the baby stirred and stretched, her fists pushing above her head and her face screwing up. Alice jumped away. Then she laughed. She scooped up her niece and held her to her chest. Abigail sat on the bed, her legs folded under her, holding her head in her hands. Her body shook in a sob.

"It's alright, Abigail. Look. She's fine."

Abigail heaved, trying to control herself. "All I could think about was …"

"Mother and Father?"

"No, the Cooper baby back in Pennsylvania."

Alice thought for a moment. "Oh, yeah. I'd forgotten about that." She had been barely older than a baby herself when the baby a few houses down from them was smothered while she napped with her mother one July afternoon. "You're just going to have to be more careful."

Abigail shook her head.

"Lay her in her bassinet when you're tired."

"I will."

Abigail pushed herself to the edge of the bed. "You rest. I'll take care of Josie until she wants to eat again," Alice said. Abigail didn't argue, just fell back onto the bed.

Alice put Josie in her bassinet downstairs as she finished gathering their dirty clothes. She kept her nearby in the shade where she could see her as she scrubbed on the washboard and hung the garments. She looked at her niece, playing quietly with one of the boys' old rattles, and feeling grateful she was well, thought, *Looks like you'll be coming to town with me from now on.* Again, she felt conflicted. Resentful and angry she was left with the burden of caring for Abigail's child, but happy and vindicated that Josie seemed to prefer her aunt to her own mother.

CHAPTER SIX

Thursday, July 16, 1863

It was just six o'clock in the evening in mid-July. There was still almost two hours of daylight left, but it was dreary with heavy rain and temperatures cooler than normal. If she hadn't known better, she'd fear it might snow. Alice read, wrapped in a blanket next to a window. She heard a knock at the door. They weren't expecting anyone, so Alice peeked through the window next to the door to see who was there. She recognized Mr. Andresen and opened the door. His eyes were open wide and rain dripped off his black leather hat. He removed the hat and water trickled out of it like the milk Josie would pour out of her tin cup to signal she was done with her meal.

"May I help you?" Alice asked.

"I have something I need to show Mrs. Stevenson."

Alice could see the edge of a newspaper peeking out underneath Mr. Andresen's coat.

"Come in." She held the door open.

Mr. Andresen stepped in and wiped his feet on the rag rug in front of the door. Alice called up the stairs behind her, "Abigail, there's someone here to see you."

Dread began to rise in Alice's throat. She had a notion of what news was coming, but she didn't dare say the words out loud to Abigail.

"Who is it?" Alice heard the words muffled by the floor above her head.

Alice hesitated. "Mr. Andresen!" She stepped aside as Abigail came down the stairs and approached.

"What is it?" Abigail asked.

Mr. Andresen didn't say anything, just handed her the wrinkled newspaper with lowered eyelids, stepping out the door.

"Thank you," Abigail mumbled, closing the door.

Alice followed Abigail into the kitchen. She put the paper down on the table and went toward the stove. Alice picked it up and read Marshall's name under the roll of those the government had reported as dead that day from Vicksburg, Mississippi. Even though she had been correct about the news, she didn't know what to say. She wanted to say the newspaper could be wrong, but she hadn't heard that to be the case with any of the other rolls. Alice watched Abigail stoke the stove's fire and place the morning's coffee on top.

Abigail said, "Marshall's dead," without a bit of detectable emotion.

"Yes," Alice whispered. "I'm sorry." She felt ridiculous apologizing. Marshall's death was also her own loss, but that was just what people said to each other when someone they were close to passed on. "What should we do?"

"I don't know," Abigail said, pulling two coffee mugs toward the front of the counter. "I suppose have some coffee and think."

"Alright." Alice got the leftover milk from the cellar and the china sugar bowl decorated with tiny blue flowers that Marshall's aunt had sent to them for a wedding gift from the cupboard. She set them on the table and sat as her sister brought the reheated coffee over, holding the pot with a grayed towel. It was only one of the first cups of coffee Alice had ever drank. She added milk and sugar, took a sip, and then added more sugar to make it more delectable and more milk to sooth the blister forming from when she burned the roof of her mouth on the first sip.

Alice thought back to what they had done when their parents had died. It had been so chaotic with the tornado damage that most of what they did didn't apply to the current situation. She remembered that on the Tuesday evening after her parents had been buried, they wrote letters to their family back east to tell them of the news.

"I suppose there are people we should inform," Alice said.

"Yes." Abigail rubbed her forehead with her index fingers. "Most of his family is in Cedar Rapids. He wrote down the addresses for me before he left, in case…" Abigail sipped coffee. "I think they are written on a folded piece of paper in the bureau in the drawer next to the bed."

"I'll go see." Alice went upstairs, using a lamp to light her way in the darkened hallways. She saw her sister and brother-in-law's bed, not even slept in enough by him to form a permanent indentation. The quilt sewn from snippets of red and blue patterned pieces of cloth between bright white scraps was pulled taut. Alice tried to be quiet so as not to wake Josie, sleeping in her crib on the other side of the room.

Alice opened the bureau drawer; it scratched and skipped. She looked toward Josie, hoping the noise didn't wake her, but the little girl was fast asleep. *Will she ever even understand what it means to have her father die?* Alice wondered.

She pulled Marshall's small Bible out of the drawer and a folded piece of paper fell to the floor. Abigail set her lamp on the bureau and unfolded the paper, seeing it contained a list of addresses in Cedar Rapids. She wasn't sure why, but emotion overcame Alice at that moment. She sat down on her sister's bed and let the tears slip down her cheeks. *My parents never got to rest in this bed and now Marshall never will again, either*. The extreme pain she felt confused her. She'd only known Marshall for a couple of years before he went away to fight in the war. He wasn't her husband; he was only her brother-in-law.

Alice wiped her eyes with her sleeve and took a few deep breaths. *I need to be strong for my sister*, she thought, *though I don't know why. She seems to be taking it well.*

Before rejoining Abigail in the kitchen, Alice took letter paper, ink, and a pen from the small desk in the sitting room. "I found the list," she said, smoothing the paper filled with the addresses onto the table in front of Abigail. "Would you like me to write any of them?"

"No, I'll do it," Abigail said. "It's my place."

"What can I do?"

"I don't know."

"What about a funeral?"

"We have nothing to bury."

"We could do something."

"You're right. Let me write these letters and we'll think of something."

Alice watched Abigail's hand fly over the paper, imagining how she was explaining the news of Marshall's death to his parents and loved ones back in Cedar Rapids. She only paused to take a drink of coffee or dip her nib for fresh ink.

Hours passed, but it was still the thick dark of night. They heard Josie's cries from upstairs and looked at the four-time drained coffee pot between them. Abigail stood her pen in the ink bottle, pushed her chair out from the table, and went upstairs. Alice followed her.

Picking her baby up, Abigail said, "Come to Mamma, sweetie."

Alice watched Abigail's eyes as she talked to her daughter as if she were old enough to understand. "I know this is going to be hard for you. But your daddy has gone to heaven."

Alice's throat tightened, remembering the moment she'd learned her own parents had died, and she waited for a sign of any tears from Abigail so she could let those dammed at the back of her throat free. But Abigail was stoic, whether acted or genuine. Josie just shook her head, babbling, and sank into her mother's lap. "You're a sleepy girl. Why don't you let Aunt Alice take you back to bed so you can get your sleep?" She kissed Josie's head through her tangled hair.

Alice picked Josie up and hugged her tightly. As she tucked her niece into her crib, she thought about how perhaps Abigail already realized Josie's father's death wasn't the same as their own father's. Josie had never met her father and only knew him by his likeness and the occasional letter Abigail shared with her, and for those she was so young, she wouldn't even remember them. She wasn't attached to him in the least and wouldn't even notice he was gone. Nothing would change for her. Maybe that's why Abigail seemed so emotionless, too. Perhaps she was already accustomed to life without her husband.

As she tucked the blankets around Josie's chin, Alice wondered why her sister even bothered to tell Josie about Marshall's passing. She wouldn't know the difference and was too young to remember it. But she supposed Abigail thought that was what she should do.

She returned to Abigail and sat quietly as Abigail wrote, waiting for her sister to need her for something. After a while, she rested her head on her outstretched arm on the tabletop. She dozed and woke to find Abigail sleeping, her cheek pressed against a short stack of addressed envelopes. It was beginning to lighten outside. Alice could see the dawn's soft blue illuminating the horizon. She tried to remove the letters from under Abigail's head without waking her, but she snapped up, backwards letters on her cheek from where she'd fallen asleep before the ink dried.

"I'll mail these when the post office opens," Alice said. She counted the correct change from the can in the cupboard, enough to purchase five stamps, and readied them on the table. She sent Abigail to bed. She waited until the sun rose a little higher in the sky. The others were still sleeping and she knew the post office wouldn't be open, but she couldn't wait and left anyway.

When she got back, the younger children were sitting at the kitchen table eating their breakfast. The boys' eyes were red and the plates in front of them essentially full, but Josie, not understanding what had happened, gurgled happily.

"Are you hungry?" Abigail asked. "There's more oatmeal."

"No, thank you. My stomach feels a little sick."

"It's probably because the only thing that has been in it is all that coffee. Have a little something." Abigail shuffled things around in the cupboard. "A few crackers?"

"Alright." Abigail sat the crackers in front of Alice. She took one and nibbled on the corner. It tasted dry and stale, but the salt calmed her stomach.

"So few people here knew Marshall, so I don't think a traditional funeral service would be appropriate. We'll have our own ceremony here. We'll paint a rock as a memorial to place in the backyard. We'll go after breakfast to find one."

It took two days for the paint to dry on the rock Abigail found and had the boys and Alice haul to the house. Under overcast skies and low-hanging clouds rolling overhead, they used a towel to slide the rock to the far northeast corner of the yard. Abigail read passages from the Bible. Alice remembered when the one was read at the funeral for the tornado victims, her parents included, and she started to cry. As Abigail closed the Bible after reading the last scripture, the clouds broke and the sun shone through with a single ray lighting up Marshall's name, birth date, and death year painted in bright green on the rock, marking his makeshift grave.

Josie stood between Alice and her mother during the informal funeral service with Samuel and David on the opposite side of the memorial rock. Josie stood quietly for a few minutes, holding Alice's hand and looking up at the underside of the linen-covered Bible from which Abigail read. It didn't take long before the stillness became too much for the little girl. First, despite Alice's efforts to regrasp it, she pulled her hand from Alice's. Then she plopped to the ground, folding her legs beneath her. She dropped her chin into her hand with her elbow resting on her knee, rolled her eyes, made a circle with her lips, and blew out with a loud whoosh. It was all Alice could do to not laugh, but she didn't dare. Abigail insisted on impeccable manners from her younger siblings in such solemn occasions and in public in general. Alice thought she was so adamant about it because she was afraid any misbehavior would be taken as a sign she wasn't caring for them properly. So Alice sucked her lips in between her teeth and bit down on them from the inside to hold in her laughter.

It was only Saturday, but Abigail insisted they observe the day in quiet. Alice dreaded how antsy she knew the children would get not being able to expend their energy for two days in a row. Abigail spent the day alternating between sitting in front of the fireplace, extinguished until autumn, and on the front porch. The weight of all they'd lost loomed over Alice and she realized there would be no reprieve; there would not be a day when Marshall would return, relieving her of the responsibilities of caring for a house and three children. Would Abigail ever be strong enough to act as the parent on her own? Alice fell asleep imagining herself in the seat of an extravagant carriage, resting her cheek against the soft sleeve on a strong arm.

*****

Alice sat next to Abigail on the front porch, their chairs, Abigail's rocking and Alice's static, angled toward each other so they could almost touch feet if they'd wanted to. Alice squinted at her needlepoint and counted the red half Xs of thread to make sure she had enough to create an apple of the correct width. Marshall had not been dead a month and they had known about it less than a week, and Alice noticed Abigail's strange behavior. Alice watched hers sister out of the corner of her eye as Abigail darned the twins' socks. She fell silent and seemed to go far away. She started talking, but Alice felt she would have kept talking even if she'd walked away. Words tumbled out of her mouth, not directed at anyone.

"Why did he leave?"

"Who?"

Abigail jumped and turned her head toward Alice.

"You asked, 'Why did he leave?'" Alice said.

Turning her face toward town, Abigail again drifted off. "I don't know why Joseph left. Perhaps that last day when he told me he was going, I angered him somehow. He said he'd come to tell me goodbye. But that was before I ran away. I was so angry. I should've been more understanding. I should've ran back to him."

Alice said, "It was understandable for you to be angry. He sprang the news on you rather suddenly, didn't he?"

"I suppose." Abigail shook her head. "I know what you must be thinking. You're thinking I'm a terrible wife because I'm more worried about where my old beau is than that my husband is dead."

Alice was silent.

"I know it's terrible of me, but I think if only I knew why, I could move on. I thought it was because he was in trouble, that he had something to do with Marty Cranson's death, but when Pamela confessed, I knew that wasn't the reason. The only reason can be that he didn't love me after all. But why? What did I do? What did I say? I keep replaying every moment we spent together in my head, trying to find that moment when everything changed. Am I mad?"

Abigail again turned toward Alice, who could feel her sister expecting an answer. "It's been a hard time for all of us," Alice said. "Perhaps you should get some sleep and you'll feel better in the morning."

"Perhaps," Abigail said, rubbing her eyes. She dropped her darning in the basket next to her chair and shuffled up the stairs.

Alice reached the end of the row at the widest part of the apple she was creating with her thread and realized she was off by two stitches. She pulled the row out to start over, feeling confused. She thought perhaps her sister *was* mad. She certainly behaved differently than all the other women with husbands fighting in the war or who were widowed by it. As she sat staring into the night air, Alice felt like a heavy rocked descended on her. There was always so much to do. The one failed stitch was the first she'd been able to attempt in weeks. Between the boys and Josie, they always needed something, and Abigail was usually in no position to get it for them. Alice tried to be understanding; Abigail was in mourning, after all, but it was beginning to wear on her. *If only I could run away*. But she had no money, no place to run away to. What options were there for an almost 13-year-old girl away from home? The only one she could think of was a husband. The demands on her wouldn't end with a husband, but they would be reduced to one person, until she had a child. But at least then it would be her own child to care for.

CHAPTER SEVEN

Saturday, August 22, 1863

It was Saturday and the hot, wet air blew up the hill and into Alice's face. Saturday was not usually washing day, but with the baby's clothes, clothes of two rambunctious boys as well as Alice's and Abigail's, one day of washing usually wasn't sufficient. Though it was early, the sun had been up for hours. Alice awoke early so she could scrub in the coolest part of the day and get the clothes hung as early as possible, since she knew it would take all day for them to dry in the humid air. Plus, Abigail had promised her she'd come straight home after working in the store so Alice could go to the ice cream social in town.

Alice rushed to get the last garment hung, knowing the boys and Josie would wake up soon, demanding breakfast.

The temperature climbed quickly. Alice fed the children cold biscuits and butter for breakfast. It was too hot for the twins to play, so they spent most of the day sitting in a tree's shade as far in the open as they could get so they could enjoy maximum breeze. They read picture books, and Alice napped briefly while Samuel and David made up stories for Josie, looking at the pictures.

Alice had a cool bath ready to jump into as soon as Abigail arrived home from the store at 4:30. She washed her hair and turned it into a tight twist, pinning it in place. She dried her body and moved slowly to keep herself dry, dusting her skin with body powder. Abigail had not used her perfume in many months, so Alice borrowed it without asking, figuring she wouldn't miss a spritz or two. She walked slowly to town and the ice cream social to make sure her perfume was the overriding scent her friends would smell. The event was held in the church yard for the congregation's young people. They explained it as a time for the young people to get together outside of their normal Sunday school and worship services, but Alice knew it was really more of a bribe to get them to continue attending services on Sundays.

Alice carefully ate her ice cream, taking small bites and turning the spoon upside down in her mouth to get all the cold vanilla cream off the underside. She noticed the boys paid attention to her. She remembered how not too long ago, she barely noticed they were there, and didn't notice until Abigail would pout, finally admitting after some prodding that she didn't like how the boys ignored her but paid so much attention to her younger sister, who wasn't old enough and didn't care. She sat on a blanket in the grass under a tree with her legs tucked to her side. Two boys came up to talk to her. One was blond, his hair slicked to the side and secured behind his ears. The other had hair and eyes nearly the identical shade of brown. They introduced themselves as Joshua Culbertson and Winston Martin.

"We haven't seen you at a social yet this summer," the blond Joshua said.

"I'm usually taking care of my little brothers or my niece."

"That hardly seems fair. Why's that?"

"I live with my widowed sister, so that's just the way it is."

"I'm joining up as soon as I'm old enough," the brown-haired Winston said. "Just got one more year to go. How old are you?"

Alice hesitated. Should she tell them the truth? "I'm almost 16," she lied. She didn't know why she lied; she'd hardly cared before if a boy thought she was older than she was, but for some reason, it seemed important.

"If the war goes on long enough," Joshua said. "I think we'll beat those rebs before that." Joshua reached over and stroked Alice's braid. "That's some pretty hair you have."

"Thanks," she replied, nervous and excited at the same time.

"So'd your sister's husband die in honor or did he just get sick?"

Joshua put his hands in his pockets. "Don't mind him. He can be a varmint. Leave her alone," he said.

"No, it's alright," Alice said. "I don't know what you mean by honor, but he died at Vicksburg early last month."

Joshua moved closer to Alice, resting his hand on the small of her back. "I'm real sorry," he said. "We'll get those gray coats in line, you'll see."

Alice shook her head, not knowing how the war's outcome would affect anything about Marshall's death. Joshua must've took her silence as encouragement because he winked at her, saying, "I'll see you again real soon" as he walked away. As Alice watched him go, she wondered if he might be her way to freedom.

*****

"Would you like to go for a ride in my carriage?" Joshua asked Alice as she walked out of church. She walked past him and around the side of the building.

"What are you doing here?" she asked.

"We had such a nice time yesterday afternoon, I thought we could spend some more time together."

Alice peeked around the corner to make sure her siblings were still speaking with the reverend and that busybody, Deedra Mahoney, wasn't lurking on her usual quest to find gossip to spread. She looked into his green-flecked eyes and her heart skipped. "I'll meet you at the Cutler warehouse in half an hour. I need to do something first."

Alice waited until Joshua turned the corner onto the street before she came out from her hiding place. Then she peeked around the corner to see her brothers bound down the church stairs, with Abigail behind, finishing her conversation with the reverend. *That was close*, Alice thought. *She didn't see.*

Putting her most solemn look on her face, Alice approached Abigail. "I've decided to take a walk. You go on home with the boys and I'll be there before supper."

"But Mrs. Alban invited us over for lunch and cookies. She'll be disappointed." Abigail thrust Josie toward Alice, but she tried to ignored her.

Alice gently pushed the child back toward Abigail. "I don't feel much like company." She pointed at her brothers. "You boys can have my cookies, all right?" The mention of extra cookies sent the boys running toward Mrs. Alban's.

"I guess we're on our way," Abigail called, rushing to catch up with them, steadying Josie against her hip. "Enjoy your walk. Don't be too late."

Alice found Joshua sitting on a bench, his horses, attached to his carriage, tethered to a cast iron spike driven into a boulder. Alice cleared her throat to get his attention.

"There she is! Beautiful day, isn't it? Are you ready for our ride?"

"I am," Alice said, grinning. She let Joshua hold her elbow as she climbed into the carriage's passenger seat.

"What's your pleasure?"

"I haven't been to Clinton in a long while. Can we drive toward there?"

"Sounds delightful," Joshua said, laughing. He joked all the way to Clinton. Alice laughed so hard, her sides hurt. They followed the Mississippi, keeping it on the carriage's right.

Over the next couple of weeks, Alice snuck away as much as she could to see Joshua, including two hours one afternoon, sipping lemonade with him down by the river. Joshua was fun. He liked to joke, and Alice couldn't remember another stretch of time she'd laughed so hard. And he was handsome with his wavy brown hair. He worked in Mr. Anthony's and Mr. McCloskey's lumber mill, so his arms were muscular, and his chest rippled underneath his twill shirt. She didn't care for Joshua in her heart but enjoyed his company.

Alice started to think about having a life with Joshua, doing her best to delay children so she could leisurely take care of him. But she quickly realized Joshua wasn't ready for such seriousness and responsibility, and over the next couple of weeks, she noticed herself laughing less and less, and Joshua became increasingly quiet. Alice peeked out the window after church and, seeing him there waiting again, she remained in her pew, pretending to study a passage in the Bible. After several minutes, Samuel and David came bounding into the church.

"Alice, come on!" Samuel said. "Abigail says we need to go home."

Alice looked out the window once again. Joshua was still there. "I'm coming," she said, taking as much time as she could to gather her things. She joined her sister and they started walking toward home. Alice didn't get far before starting to feel guilty for not even glancing Joshua's way as she left the church. She stopped and pretended to look in her purse. "Oh, Abigail, I forgot my hymnal. I need to go back."

"Alright. We'll wait for you."

"No, I've already held you up long enough. Go on ahead and I'll catch up." She walked back to the church to find Joshua sitting cross-legged on the ground beneath the tree.

He stood up as he saw her approach. "Good morning. I was beginning to think you wouldn't be able to get away today."

"I can't. I just came back to tell you. I promised to spend the afternoon with my family. They say I've been neglecting them."

"Alright. But I did need to speak to you about something important."

"What is it?"

Joseph looked around the tree. "I'd planned for a prettier spot, but I suppose it doesn't matter." He dropped to one knee. *Oh no*, Alice thought. "I … I was wondering … or I hoped … or … will you be my wife?"

Alice shook her head. *What am I going to do?* she thought. *This has gone way too far.*

"Do you need some time to think?"

"No."

"Oh," Joshua said, his face falling.

"I can't," Alice said.

"I see."

"I like you. And we've had fun. But …"

Joshua interrupted. "No, it's alright. I understand. I just thought it couldn't hurt to ask," he said, smiling.

"I suppose not. I'm sorry."

"No need."

They stood in awkward silence.

"I should be going," Alice said. "They're going to wonder where I've disappeared to."

"Yes, me too. I should be going." He held out his hand toward Alice. "It was fun. Maybe I'll see you in town sometime."

Alice took his hand, shook it, and curtseyed. "Yes." She waved as she walked away. As she rushed toward home, she thought about how breaking things off with Joshua was easier than she'd thought it would be. At first, his sad look made her pity him, but in the end, he took it well. Alice decided it was rather amusing to spend some time with a man, enjoy the trinkets he bought for her, and then move on when things got too serious. She did love her family, so perhaps leaving wasn't the answer, but an occasional distraction to make the work more bearable.

As Alice began to gather the family's clothes to do yet more laundry, Abigail stopped her, taking the garments from her hands. "No, we must stop this. It's the Lord's day. It's sacrilegious to be working." Something Reverend said must've gotten to her.

"Are you going to help me clean them tomorrow, then?" Alice asked.

Abigail nodded in agreement, but Alice doubted her sincerity. That afternoon, she sat on the porch trying to read the Bible, but her mind kept drifting away. She hoped she hadn't hurt Joshua's feelings too badly; after she'd turned him down, he smiled and laughed like it had all been a joke, and Alice wondered if it was. She watched her sister rocking her niece and her brothers playing quietly in the grass. *This isn't so bad. But I did enjoy Joshua. I'll just need to be more careful and not let my future beaus get too serious.*

PART TWO

CHAPTER EIGHT

Thursday, April 27, 1865

During her errands on Thursday afternoons, Alice always happened by the boarding
houses or ate a snack by the river where the single men spent their time after work fishing for
catfish. She flirted with a few of the men, but did
her best to keep her distance. When they asked
her to dinner on Saturday nights or to ride with
them on Sunday afternoons, she created excuses,
hesitant to risk allowing any of them to get as serious as Joshua. She'd back away if ever they
tried to touch her arm or her hair or hold her hand,
telling herself that she was still being honorable
and not leading them on. That she was just making friends. She started to see a man out of the

corners of her eyes when she'd go on her excursions. She noticed him watching her talk to the bachelors, grinning slightly and shaking his head like he was amused by something.

One day, one of the single men noticed that Alice was distracted and said, "He's quite new in town. William Anderson, I believe, is his name."

Alice snapped her attention back. "Oh. I've noticed him a few times. He always seems to be lurking around."

"He's shy, I think."

In town, Alice began to get a warm feeling in her stomach, and when she turned around, William Anderson was always somewhere nearby. She'd deliberately walk past him, so close that he couldn't politely ignore her. He tipped his hat, smiled, and bowed his head, but didn't say a word. Alice's heart pounded. Finally, her answer to his insolence and her curiosity got the better of her.

She walked up to him, stuck her hand out, and said, "Good afternoon. I'm Alice Sinkey. How do you do?"

He stood up and his eyes seemed to sparkle. He took her hand and brought the back of it to his lips. Alice felt sizzling bolts travel up her arm.

"The name's William Anderson, ma'am. It's a pleasure to meet you."

"You're not from around here, are you?" Alice said, suddenly realizing the familiarity of his eyes.

"No, ma'am. I've come up this way from Tennessee. I'm here because my older cousin told me about the pretty river and ample work availability, so I thought I'd give it a try."

"Who's your cousin?"

"James Mackenrow. Our mothers are sisters. His was the eldest sister and mine was the youngest. Are you acquainted?"

"Yes. I went to school with his daughter, Lucy."

"Then you know what's happened with his wife?"

Alice wrapped her arms around her waist. "I do."

"He doesn't like to talk about it much. And neither does Lucy. Of course, they are both so busy, there hasn't been much time for visiting. I'm not much for talking anyway, so I don't mind."

"Nobody likes to talk about it much."

"Very well. So what do folks around here talk about?"

Alice laughed. "Usual things. The weather. Crops."

"What do you like to talk about?"

She was quiet, thinking. What did she like to talk about? She talked about many things with Abigail, but couldn't say whether or not she liked discussing them. She could feel her face turning red. She bowed her head and looked through her eyelashes out the top of her eyes at him. "You must think I'm dreadfully silly. I cannot think of a single thing I like to talk about."

"How about when you get together with the ladies? You know, for those quilting bees and canning parties and such."

"I'm afraid I don't participate in those too much. I'm normally too busy taking care of my little brothers and niece or doing housework. Or running errands, which is what I'm usually doing when I'm in town."

William leaned against a fence post. He pushed his hair back and put his hat on over it. "Yes, I've noticed you completing your *errands*," he said.

Alice's face burned even hotter. "I … I . . ."

Laughing and crossing his right leg over his left, he said, "Don't worry. I don't think ill of you. Which one of them is your beau?"

"None." Alice dismissed them by waving her arm. "They are just my friends. It gets old only talking to my brothers and sister, and my sch… my other friends are busy with chores and beaus."

"I see." Williams eyes were sparkling again. *Did he read my thoughts? Is he going to ask me how old I am now?* But he didn't ask, and she didn't offer.

Alice found herself looking for William on her trips to town, and she always found him. He didn't meet her after church like Joshua did, but when she walked by his place, he was there, waiting with his carriage. Abigail had begun to question Alice about her mental state, asking if she was well and if she wanted to talk about anything. So she had to change tactics, saying she was spending time with various friends she hoped Abigail never spoke to instead of saying she needed time alone to walk. Though William was open and animated with her, he admitted it was an unusual state for him, and this made her feel special.

*****

It had been exactly five years since that terrible day, June 3, 1860; half a decade that Alice had been living without her parents. She was 15 and a half, and her twin brothers were no longer babies at eight years old. As evening approached, she couldn't help letting her mind wander back to the moments five years ago. The weather wasn't that much different, though the air seemed to have weighed much heavier that day.

Alice remembered she'd played tag in the yard with Samuel and David. She was "it" but didn't try too hard. The air was hot and sticky, and she didn't like to sweat. Alice vaguely thought that she had gotten the stick's short end again, stuck watching her brothers while Abigail read under a tree in the yard. Of course, after Joseph broke off their engagement, they'd all been tiptoeing around her so they didn't make her cry again, and Alice didn't dare complain about getting stuck watching her brothers.

Samuel walked up to Alice. "What are you doing? I'm going to get you and you'll be it," Alice said.

"I'm thirsty," Samuel said.

David was hiding around the house's corner. "David, come on, Samuel's thirsty. We're going to get a drink."

Alice refilled the water bucket with fresh water from the pump and took it into the cabin to get their cups. She'd filled the boys' and was just about to fill hers with the ladle when Abigail burst in through the door.

Out of breath, Abigail said, "Tor…na…do! Come on! Cellar!" Alice looked up, stunned, and could see that behind Abigail the sky had turned orange. Abigail said, "You get David. I'll grab Samuel."

Alice chased Samuel under the kitchen table. Abigail caught hold of David's arm before he could join him. They pulled the boys to the front door. Alice couldn't see the storm, but she could feel it getting closer. The world had turned dark, looking more like late than early evening. The horizon seemed to rumble in the distance. Abigail's black braid whipped in the wind. Alice worked to push her blonde hairs that scattered and fanned across her face like a spider web away so she could see where she was going. Alice held tightly to David's hand and followed Abigail, carrying Samuel to the nearly constructed house.

Abigail lifted the heavy cellar door on the side. She pushed the boys in.

David tripped down the last two stairs. "Ouch!" he said and examined the new scrape on his knee. Samuel tumbled over him in a somersault.

"Get to the corner. Get as far back as you can," Abigail said.

"But it's yucky," Alice said.

"Just do it. Hurry!"

Abigail pushed the boys and Alice toward the back of the cellar and into the jars of canned tomatoes and pickles, which rocked and rattled but didn't fall over. The dust swirled as it was stirred up by the gust of wind that came in as they opened the door. Abigail pushed the children to the floor. Alice sat cross-legged with Samuel and David on each knee. She hugged them close to her. The cellar door behind Abigail started to shake.

"I want Mother," Samuel said.

"I want Father," David said.

Alice said, "Everything will be alright," trying to believe her own words.

"Stay there," Abigail said.

Though she'd tried not to, Alice started crying. She tried to do it quietly, hoping the boys couldn't hear her.

Abigail said, "Don't come out until I come to get you. I'm going to find Mother and Father."

She left, letting the door slam behind her. The cellar door shook some more, but then it suddenly went quiet. There hardly seemed to be a breath of air, but Alice did what she was told, waiting for Abigail to return in the dark, holding on to her twin brothers. A thin line of light appeared around the cellar door's edges, but still Abigail didn't return. Alice dozed.

In the dark, Alice heard Abigail. "Where are you?" She squinted to try to see her in the darkness, and her eyes adjusted to the moon illuminating the night.

"Abigail?" Alice said. She held Samuel and David under each of her arms like sacks of potatoes. She set them down at Abigail's feet and threw her arms around her waist. Abigail pushed her away and crouched in front of her.

She said, "Are you all right? Are you hurt?"

Alice patted her chest and skirts. "I think I'm all right. Samuel?"

Alice patted Samuel all over while Abigail did the same to David. "Nothing feels broken," she said. "Are you hurt?" David shook his head. "Samuel?"

"I think they're fine," Alice said.

Her sister grabbed Alice's hand. She took Samuel's, who took David's hand in his, and Abigail pulled them all out of the root cellar in a chain. They looked together at the house, still holding hands. It was in one piece but damaged. Its wood shingles were strewn in a path over the hill.

David whimpered.

"Come on, we have to find Mother and Father." Alice huddled with the twins while Abigail found and lit a lantern to light the way. They cut to the right, around town, through the brush toward the river, and Alice wondered why they were taking such a long path. They walked hand-in-hand. Alice scanned the debris scattered everywhere. She followed pieces of furniture, fabric, and wood with her eyes, mangled around naked trees and among dead livestock. Abigail steered them around a dead pig and then stopped abruptly.

She dropped Alice's hand and said, "Stay here."

Abigail ran toward a pile of clothes in the distance, tripping on her skirts. Alice watched Abigail sink to her knees in front of the pile, and as Alice approached, she saw her sister sinking in the mud, rocking back and forth, holding her stomach with clenched fists.

Abigail looked up and said, "Stay back! Don't come any closer."

"Why? The twins want Mother," Alice said, realizing the pile of clothes were her parents. She stood staring at them with her brothers. Abigail grabbed her shoulder and turned their bodies toward home. She said, "Come on. I need a sheet."

Alice started to whimper, the full realization that her parents were dead hitting her in the gut. But she didn't want to believe it. "A sheet? Why?" she asked. Abigail didn't answer.

When they got home, Abigail sat them down in the grass away from the house. She went into the cabin but came out moments later. Alice started to get up, but Abigail said, "Stay there. Keep the twins and stay there." They walked back to where their parents lay, but Abigail wouldn't let them get too close. Alice watched her sister cover her mother and father with the sheet with wide eyes. Her mouth hung open. Then she dropped her head to her chest and allowed the sobs to possess and shake her body. Alice sat down cross-legged in front of them, facing Alice. She pulled Samuel and David into her, reaching her arms around them and Alice.

"It's going to be all right," she said.

"When is Mother coming home?" David asked.

Abigail sat the boys down on either side of Alice and looked from one to the other, directly into their eyes. "Mother and Father are not coming home," she said. "They went to live with God in Heaven. Remember how we learned about that in church?

"Who will take care of us?" Samuel said.

"I'm the oldest, so it's my job. Just like it has always been my job to take care of you when Mother and Father are not at home. And Alice will take care of you, and I will take care of Alice, too."

Alice slowly lifted her head. "But who will take care of you?" she asked.

Abigail whispered, "I will."

The next day, so much had changed; so much would never be the same. And now, even more had changed. Marshall, her brother-in-law who'd allowed them to stay at their home and helped them to finish building the house, was gone. One thing hadn't changed, though. *I still work my skin off most every day*, Alice thought as she pulled the broom over the rough floors.

She remembered how upset Abigail had been when Joseph broke off their engagement to return home to Ohio to help his ailing parents; she'd sulked all day and nothing anyone did could cheer her up. They finally just left her alone. Her parents went for a walk and Alice played with the boys, leaving Abigail to sit under a tree to read.

While he was courting Abigail, Joseph had seemed nice enough, and he seemed to care about her sister, but ever since he broke off their engagement, a ball of distrust for Joseph started to grow in Alice's mind. When he never stopped over to say goodbye and never wrote Abigail a letter, even after surely hearing about the tornado that was covered in newspapers across the country, she had no use for him. To her, he was a coward, and she couldn't understand why Abigail still pined for him.

As Alice thought of her parents, her mind turned toward beaus. The thought of taking care of one man rather than three siblings and a niece made her anxious. Then her mind circled back to her parents. Hard as she tried, she realized every memory of their faces came from their photographs. She squinted her eyes, and tried to picture them, alive and animated. She finally brought their smiles as they waved before leaving on their walk that terrible day into focus, holding it in her imagination as she fell asleep, vowing to never forget.

CHAPTER NINE

Friday, August 4, 1865

"It feels like it's going to be hot again to-day," Alice said, trying to break the heavy tension weighing on the breakfast table. They had adjusted to life after war as best they could, and usually the mornings were filled with the children's chatter. The war had left many of their friends and neighbors surviving without their husbands, brothers, and sons, just like them, and President Lincoln had been killed, but there was a relief that there would be no more war killing, and the days took on some degree of normalcy.

They'd heard about the problems happening in the South, and they were glad they weren't there. Many Union troops were still there, trying to calm the unrest and change the social and political institutions. Some people the Southerners menacingly called carpetbaggers went to take personal advantage of the situation. The Freedman's Bureau had been set up to help freed slaves live on their own, but some Southerners were against that, even forming a group called the Ku Klux Klan.

Alice dropped her fork on her plate. She watched Abigail jump. She looked at her nervously but didn't say anything. *What is the matter with her?* Alice wondered as she watched Abigail pick at her eggs.

Finally, Abigail spoke. "We're going to have a guest for supper tonight," she said.

Alice looked up from her plate. When Abigail didn't meet her eyes, she said, "Who?"

Abigail cleared her throat. "Joseph Sund."

Alice's eyes widened so far she feared they would pop out into her eggs. "Why?"

"He's back in town and wanted to see everyone again."

Alice couldn't believe Abigail's calm demeanor. *After all the lamenting she's done about Joseph, why he left, why he didn't write, why this and why that, and now she just announces him coming to supper as casually as if it was Mrs. Alban joining them.*

"What did he say?" Alice asked. "Why did …"

"That's between him and me."

"That's not fair. After all you've talked about him with me, you won't tell me the answer to the big question you always ask?"

Abigail picked up the boys' empty plates. "I know. I'm sorry. It was a misunderstanding. He did send me a letter after the tornado, but I never received it. Since I never responded, he thought that I was too angry with him."

"But why now? Why did he decide to come back here now?"

"He was mustered out of the infantry and wanted to know for sure, I suppose."

"What does he want from you?"

"I think he just wants to apologize. After that, I'm sure he'll move on. Something about the war made him need to revisit his past, I suppose."

But Alice could tell there was more to it than that; there was a hint of hope in Abigail's words.

The clock on the parlor fireplace mantel chimed 5:00 just as Alice heard a knock at the door and then the loud footsteps of one of her brothers racing down the stairs. Alice glared at Abigail as she led Joseph into the room. She hadn't appreciated the request to sit and make conversation with Joseph while Abigail finished supper. She noticed yellow coneflowers in his hands; his hair was combed to the side and slicked down. *He's only here to apologize and move on?*

Samuel reached for the flowers, but Abigail pushed him away. He stepped back, laughing.

"This way," Abigail said. Joseph thrust the flowers in front of her and Abigail took them. "Thank you," she said.

David stood behind Samuel, looking serious. Abigail said, "You remember Samuel and David," pointing to which twin was which. "And Alice." She swept her hand toward where Alice sat in the parlor. Josie looked up from where she was sitting on the floor playing with her doll. Abigail said to her, "And you remember Josie from when you first stopped by." Joseph nodded. "Supper's almost done. I thought you could sit in here while I finish. Would you like anything to drink?"

Joseph sat in the only remaining unoccupied chair. "Water, please."

Abigail nodded toward Alice and said, "I'll be right back."

Alice watched Josie play with her doll, wondering what Abigail expected her to say. Abigail returned quickly with the water. Alice could hear the ice clinking against the crystal as Abigail's shaking hands handed it to Joseph.

"How have you been?" Joseph asked.

How have I been? Is he mad? "Fine," Alice said. "And you?"

"I've been better lately. I had been in the war."

"Yes, I know." *Did he expect a prize?* "My brother-in-law was in the war, too. But he didn't make it back home."

"I know. I'm sorry about that. It must be difficult."

Alice nodded her head.

"What year are you in school now?"

"I'm finished. I'd thought about going back after the war, but I don't think I need to. Besides, I still haven't the time."

Alice could sense Joseph was about to ask her about any beaus or plans for matrimony and was grateful when Abigail announced supper. She hoped Abigail would call on her to set the table, but when she entered the dining room, she found the table set and the food laid out, ready for serving. They sat at their usual places with Samuel and David to Abigail's right and Alice and Josie, propped up so she could reach the table, on her left, leaving Joseph's seat at the head of the table opposite Abigail, the place occupied by the man of the house, Marshall's seat before he left, and the seat where her father would have sat had he lived to see construction completed.

Joseph clasped his hands in his lap and bowed his head. David snapped his hand back from his serving fork and they followed his lead.

"May I?" Joseph asked.

"Certainly," Abigail whispered.

Joseph recited the blessing and they began to eat.

Samuel said, "Tell us about the war."

"Boys," Abigail said, "I'm not sure that Mr. Sund wants to relive his experience."

"I don't mind," Joseph said.

"Well, it's really not appropriate table conversation anyway."

Joseph cleared his throat. "Alright. Tell me, what did you do today?" He looked around the table. "Alice?"

"Nothing worth telling," she said.

He turned toward the twins.

"Played," Samuel said. The boys and Joseph chattered through the meal. Abigail stood to gather the dishes.

"I'll clean up," Alice said.

"Are you sure?"

"I don't mind." Alice took the plate from Abigail's hands, moved close to her, and whispered, "Besides, he's *your* guest."

"All right. Thank you, Alice." Abigail turned toward the boys. "Ahem. Didn't you two say you were going to read your book this evening?"

"I did," David said, turning his head toward Samuel, who reluctantly admitted he had expressed intentions to read as well.

"Then get started, please," Abigail said.

Alice started the dishes. As she rubbed the rag over the plates in a circular motion, her movements slowed as an uneasy feeling grew in the pit of her stomach. *Why is he here? What can he possibly want?* One thing she was sure of, he wouldn't be moving on after a brief visit.

CHAPTER TEN

Tuesday, August 15, 1865

"Alice!" Alice heard the front door shut and came out to see Abigail hanging her shawl on the hook on the wall by the door. "Alice!" She turned around and jumped. "You're never going to believe it. I can't believe it."

"What is it?" Alice asked.

"Pamela Mackenrow is being released from the asylum."

"What? How?"

"I heard it in town. They said the asylum figured out she didn't kill Marty, so they're letting her come home."

"When?"

"Any minute, I suppose. Mr. Mackenrow got the news early this morning and rushed straight down there to pick her up. Did you know anything about this? Did Lucy say anything?"

"I haven't spoken to Lucy in months. This is the first I've heard anything like this." Alice chewed on her thumb nail. "If Mrs. Mackenrow didn't do it, then who did?"

Abigail shrugged her shoulders.

"Could it have been the tornado after all?"

"I don't think so. At the time, the officials seemed quite certain that it wasn't the tornado that killed Marty. There was a gunshot."

The sisters barely said two words to each other for the rest of the day and the entire evening. There was no reading the latest mystery story. There were no confessions from Abigail about Joseph, although those had dwindled considerably since Joseph had reappeared in Abigail's life. Alice kept wondering if Pamela didn't murder Marty, then who did. She wondered if the same thoughts were running through Abigail's mind as well, or if her sister was only thinking about her re-blossoming romance with Joseph. *Was Abigail wondering if it was Joseph who did it after all?*

The next morning, after tossing in her bed all night, Alice fed her brothers and Josie cold biscuits and jam, and then left them in her sister's hands as she paid a visit to Lucy. She thought of dozens of explanations of what Lucy's mother's release meant. Was she cured? How did she prove she hadn't killed Marty? And would Lucy finally forgive her family?

Alice walked up to Lucy's door but didn't knock right away. Instead, she stood thinking about what she should say after showing up suddenly the morning after her mother is exonerated from killing a man and after their relationship had been so strained for months. She got her nerve, took a deep breath, and rapped her knuckle on the repainted door. It stuck in its hinges as it opened with a lunge. Lucy peered through, looked behind her, opened the door just enough to fit, and squeezed through, closing the door behind her. Her red hair was disheveled and what wasn't covered by a folded-in-half handkerchief was covered in dust.

"Hello, Lucy."

"I can't talk. Mother and I are in the middle of deep cleaning the house."

"Apparently she didn't believe yours and your father's housekeeping skills were satisfactory?" Alice laughed, trying to lighten the mood.

"It was difficult, and no, not up to her exacting standards, I suppose."

"I'm sorry, I didn't mean …"

"What do you want?"

Alice felt defensive, like Lucy was accusing Abigail of lying or tricking Pamela into confessing all over again. "I heard that your mother was back home and I just wanted to see how you were doing. Even though we haven't been close, I still care about you."

Lucy studied the edge of the door, paint chipping after years of rubbing against the frame, seeming to contemplate whether she should slam it in Alice's face.

She sighed and said, "In her therapy at the asylum, the doctors decided that my mother didn't kill Marty Cranson after all."

"I don't understand."

"When she confessed, my mother believed she must've had shot Mr. Cranson. But after talking with the doctors, she revealed that she had passed out and didn't recall pulling the trigger. She'd just assumed she had done it. After her electroshock one day, she remembered that she'd never pulled the trigger and someone else was there."

"Who?"

"She doesn't remember. It's still fuzzy. She thinks she might know him, but she refused to accuse someone when she doesn't know for sure. She doesn't want anything to happen to anyone else like what happened to her."

"Oh." Alice stared at her feet. "It's good to have her home, though?"

"Yes. Father and I were very happy to get the news. I must get back now. We have a lot to do."

"Certainly." Alice watched Lucy disappear through the door before she turned, stepped down from the front stoop, and returned home.

CHAPTER ELEVEN

Monday, August 21, 1865

"I don't know where to go from here, Alice. When I saw him standing in the yard talking to Josie, I felt everything I'd always thought I'd feel all at once. I was relieved he was alive. Elated that he came back. In a rage because of what he'd done. And sad, too. I felt love, hate, and indifference running through me at the same time. The only thing I knew for sure was I wanted to escape. I felt like I was in a torrent I had to get away from. You're only 15; this probably makes no sense to you."

"I'll be 16 soon," Alice said. "I understand, but if it was me, I think I'd lean more toward anger after what he'd done."

Abigail leaned over the rocking chair's arm and said, "It was all a big misunderstanding. He wrote me a letter, but I never received it. Since he didn't get a response, he assumed I was too angry with him. Now I don't know what to do. It's like there is this invisible thread between us. I felt it there all the while he was gone and seeing him again only made it thicker."

"But what's stopping him from doing it again, leaving, not saying goodbye, not contacting you?"

"I am afraid of that. He promises he'd never do that again, that he's grown up since then and realized how mean he was for doing that." Abigail leaned back into her chair and sighed. "I still feel a physical pull toward him, too." She put her hands over her lower abdomen. "Whenever he's near me or I think of touching him – even just his hand – I feel warm down here."

Alice's face heated; she recognized that feeling from being around William, but propriety forbade discussing it. She watched her sister stare into a dream Alice couldn't see and thought that even though Abigail was afraid and reluctant, Joseph would win her back if that was what he decided he wanted.

*****

Summer was in full bloom, and Alice spent most of her days trying to keep her bonnet atop her head to shade her face from the blistering August sun while she gathered the garden's harvest. Her hands were crusted and blistered. She'd tried wearing gloves, but they were too hot, and as the sweat from her hands had nowhere to go, they ended up just as beat up and sore as if she hadn't worn them at all. Joseph had joined them for supper at least twice a week since he'd been back, but Abigail didn't say much about him. She just walked around with a half-smile on her face, only mentioning him when they negotiated their child-sitting duties on Friday and Saturday evenings when they each wanted to spend time away with their beaus.

Alice picked the last ripe tomato of the day and was on her way to the house to prepare them for canning the next day when she saw Joseph riding on the road toward her. *Again?* He had been there the day before for supper. It had been so hot, they had taken to eating whatever was left cooled in the cellar. *She'd better not expect me to cook a whole fancy meal again.* Alice glared toward Joseph. He waved, but she quickly looked away and pretended she didn't notice. She went into the house.

"Abigail!" she called, opening the back door. As soon as she did, she heard Josie crying. She dropped her basket on the table and went to investigate. The little girl sat on the floor, wailing and hugging her right knee where pink was starting to ooze from a small scrape. Samuel and David sat on each side of her, looking bewildered and blowing on the wound.

"Shhh," Samuel said. "You're going to get us in trouble."

"What happened?" Alice rushed to them.

"We were just playing, and she fell," David said.

"Let me see." She squeezed between her brothers. "It's not so bad. Just a little scratch." Josie hiccoughed. "It'll feel better in a minute.

Should we put a cool cloth on it?" Josie nodded her head. "Where's Abigail?" Alice asked, picking Josie up.

"Upstairs," David said.

"Getting ready," Samuel finished.

Alice rolled her eyes. She sat Josie on a kitchen chair. She poured water from the pitcher into the basin and dipped a clean washcloth in it. "What exactly were you playing?" she asked as she gently touched the cool cloth to Josie's knee. Josie flinched, but then relaxed into the treatment. Alice looked up at the boys. "Well?" They shrugged their shoulders. "What were you playing, Josie?"

"Horsey!"

"Horsey?" She gave the boys her sternest look. "You know you aren't supposed to play such rough games, especially in the house." She sat Josie down in the living room. "You two, help her keep the cloth on her knee until she feels better."

Looking through downturned eyelashes, David said, "We're sorry."

Alice messed up his hair. "I know. Don't do it again." She wasn't angry with them anyway; although they were old enough to be in charge of Josie, it was Abigail's ultimate responsibility.

As she stood, she saw Joseph standing outside the front door. *How long has he been there?* She opened the door. "Yes?"

He looked flustered. "I … I knocked, but nobody heard me, so I waited." He rocked onto his heels. "Abigail invited me to supper."

Alice waved her arm toward the middle of the room. "Come in. I hope that Abigail has a plan for supper, because I don't." She knew she was being rude but couldn't help herself.

Her rudeness continued as they ate the array of leftovers and freshly sliced tomatoes from the garden. "I saw Faith Mason in town yesterday," Alice said. "She lost her husband in the war, too." It was the only way she could think of to bring her dead brother-in-law into the conversation. She pretended to be deep in thought. "I miss Marshall," she said, dabbing the corner of her eye with her napkin. She smiled. "Do you remember the time he had the boys go sledding when there was just frost on the grass?"

The boys chattered about the memory, laughing about how they'd thought it was Christmas, but it was only a heavy, late October frost. It was cold, so they'd had church at home. Alice smiled, remembering how she'd almost refused to go out, but was glad she had because she'd had so much fun sliding down the slick grass with her brothers and Marshall.

Alice laid more diced salt pork on Josie's plate. The little girl had gotten into the habit of only eating well when Alice fed her. "It's too bad Josie will never get to know her father ..." She tried to sound wistful as she looked sideways at the rest of the table. Abigail glared at her, but Joseph's reddening face was intent on his plate and he seemed not to have heard her. *Strange*, Alice thought.

"Marshall would've been such a wonderful father," Alice said, staring as forcefully as she could at Joseph's scalawag head.

He glanced up and coughed. He took a drink of water and kept coughing. Samuel got up and pounded his back. He waved and put his fist over his mouth. He sipped more water. "I'm alright," he said.

"There was bones in it!" David said. Joseph looked at him, confused.

Alice laughed. "That was something Marshall used to say." He couldn't ignore her now. Alice didn't think his face could get any redder, but it did.

"That's a good one," Joseph finally choked out. "I'll have to remember that and check for bones."

Abigail's mouth laughed, but her eyes told Alice definitively that the discussion about her dead husband was over. For the rest of the night, Alice's thoughts kept drifting back to Joseph's reaction. She'd expected him to get embarrassed, but his reaction was so extreme, and he was careful to avoid Alice the rest of the time he was there.

*****

As Alice prepared for her evening with William on Friday, she had a nagging thought that her suitor was approaching the point where she needed to break away. But she didn't want to. William was different. He listened to her and seemed to genuinely care. When her old beaus started to hint at marriage, she immediately pulled away and broke things off, but not with William. She just pretended she didn't hear and changed the subject. She felt badly, because she knew with each hint he made, it would hurt him more when he learned she wasn't sure that was what she wanted. But she wasn't ready to let him go, and with Joseph not going away any moment soon, she was beginning to think of marriage as a real option.

As he held firmly to her elbow to help her climb in, Alice noticed William's carriage was recently cleaned. Its black paint sparkled in the late afternoon sun. Alice tucked her skirts around her legs. She noticed he wasn't quite so responsive as he usually was when she talked to him about her week of hard work. At the river, he spread a blanket and laid out his picnic.

"I'm sorry I wasn't able to bring the food," Alice said, wondering if he was reconsidering her suitability as a wife.

"No, no, it's perfectly fine," he said, holding his hand out to steady her as she sat on the blanket, her legs tucked to her side. It hurt her back to sit in such a way, but it would be improper to splay her legs out in front of her or sit with them crossed like she did when she was by herself or playing with the children.

"I just picked some ready-to-go things from the store," he said. Alice noticed an array of cheeses, meats, breads, and crackers. "I also got this," he said, pulling a bottle of red wine from his bag. "I'm sorry I don't have proper cups, though. I spent all of my money on the bottle and didn't have enough left." He pulled out two coffee mugs. "So I hope these will be alright."

Alice took one of the mugs. "These will be just fine." He filled each of their cups halfway and they sat sipping and watching the shadows reach across the river. Alice remembered her manners. "How was your week?"

As he talked about his work, Alice was only able to half-listen because she kept thinking about Joseph. *That's another thing that's strange*, she thought. *Why can't she have a proper courtship with him instead of burdening us with him on any day of the week?* She wanted to tell William about Joseph's strange behavior, but she couldn't bring herself to do it, and she didn't know why. It could've been because she thought it made her seem childish and foolish, like a jealous widow's child.

So she turned her attention back to William. He looked at her as if he'd just asked a question, but she hadn't heard it. He snapped off a tall weed beyond the blanket's edge, tearing off bits and flicking them past his shoes. "I was saying how the other day, when I came home after such a difficult day, I thought how it would be so nice to have a beautiful face to meet me at the door." He flicked the last piece of weed and turned toward Alice. He used a bent finger to pull her chin toward him and then kissed her on the cheek.

It felt warm, but she didn't know if that was from the kiss or the wine. William had always been the utmost gentleman with her and this was the first liberty he tried to take. Alice blushed and gathered her strength.

"Oh," she said, taking a deep breath. "I suppose every man would like someone to have his supper waiting for him after work."

William sighed. "Yes, but it's more than that. It would be a better evening when I didn't have to cook my own supper and wash my own clothes, certainly, but it's also about having someone there to share the time with." He was quiet for a minute. "I guess what I'm saying is that I'd like for us to be able to discuss our days with each other more than once each week."

"Oh," was all she could say.

"Perhaps once per week is all that you can put up with me." He laughed, but it sounded nervous.

The tension that had settled into her shoulder blades released. He wasn't going to propose marriage, at least not yet. "Not at all," she said. "Though I'm not sure when I'd have the time with the children and my work at home."

She noticed pleading in his eyes. "But that's part of it as well. You work too hard. You should be out having more fun. I'd like to give that to you. I love to see you smile, and it seems like it takes so long for you to let the tension from all that work leave you and let the smiles come through. I was hoping that spending more time together might help."

Alice boldly touched William's forearm. "That is very sweet of you." She left her hand resting on his arm, and he didn't make any move suggesting he didn't want it there. "How about Sunday afternoons? I will simply tell my sister that since she's decided it was sacrilegious to work on Sundays anyway, she can have Joseph over to our house instead of traipsing off with him, leaving me stuck with the children."

William beamed as he laid his hand over Alice's, brought her fingers to his lips and kissed them. "Shall we eat?"

Alice knew she had turned some sort of corner with William. She wasn't sure what, though she had a feeling it would involve more kisses. She smiled at that thought.

CHAPTER TWELVE

Saturday, September 2, 1865

Alice heard Joseph and Abigail talking on the porch below, so she opened her window wider, as quietly as she could.

She heard Joseph say, "Think about it, Abigail. Marty had a confusing past. Maybe he knew Marshall before he came to Camanche. We have no way of knowing. Perhaps he came here to get some sort of revenge. Lord knows there were plenty of people Marty wronged in his past. He could have shot Marty and was heading out of town when the tornado hit."

"But Pamela said she was with Marty when the tornado hit. That he was alive then."

"He could've came in after Pamela was knocked out, shot Marty, and got hit with something at the same time. He could've made it as far as your place, injured in the way he was, but he couldn't get any further. All he had to do was turn his body to look like he'd come from the west."

"It couldn't be," Abigail said. "It wasn't in his nature. It would've been no more in his nature to kill someone than it would be in yours."

Alice choked, and fearing they'd hear her, ducked down so she was crouching beneath her window sill, but they didn't seem to notice.

"What did you really know about him, anyway?" Joseph asked.

"I knew he came from Cedar Rapids. He left me his families' addresses before he left for the war, and I used them to let them know he'd passed, but that was it. He didn't like to talk about it very much. He used to say his life began the moment he saw me the morning after the tornado."

"There's even more proof he could've done it. It seems suspicious to me that he wouldn't talk about his past. He just showed up out of nowhere and started a life with you. Doesn't that strike you as a bit strange?"

"A little. But what does it matter? If he did it, he's gone now. He can't be punished."

"If we can prove he did it, it will prove that I didn't do it, and then any suspicion against me will be lifted."

Abigail didn't respond.

"I know that you've heard the whispers in town as much as I have," Joseph said.

"But how can we prove it?" Abigail asked.

"I don't know. We need to think of something."

Alice tried to stay awake to listen, but they didn't say anything else for a long time. She fell asleep. When she awoke, she peeked in on Abigail. She was sound asleep in her bed, and Joseph had gone.

*****

On the first Sunday after Alice made arrangements with William to spend Sunday afternoons with him, it became clear that her suspicions about his actual intentions with the request were correct. He'd asked her to marry him. It was a simple request. "I'm getting ready to go back to Tennessee soon. I wondered if you'd be willing to marry me and come with me."

Despite the nagging alarms in her head, she agreed. Alice had hoped she could enjoy a long engagement, but William seemed anxious.

"It's going to be getting colder soon, darling. We need to find a house and set up our home before it starts snowing," William said. He held Alice's hand and they walked along the Mississippi, the leaves raining down as they let loose from the trees.

"I know, but I can't leave my sister now."

"She's your older sister, Alice. She can take care of herself. I know you don't like this Joseph, but it's really her decision."

"There's more to it than that."

"Yes, and I wish you'd tell me what it is."

"I can't. Not now. Not until I know for sure."

"I thought you wanted to marry me."

"I do." Alice placed William's hand against her cheek. "She's my sister, and she's been the only one to take care of me for the past five years. I can't leave until I know she's going to be okay."

William leaned in so his chin rested against Alice's forehead. "How can I help?"

Alice backed up, her face lit. "I have an idea. You go ahead and find us a house. By then, I'm sure I'll have everything figured out. You can come back to get me, we can get married, and go back."

"I don't want to find a house without you. What if you don't like it?"

Grabbing William's arm, Alice leaned into him and pulled him along to walk beside her. "Don't worry about that. I'm not fussy. And you know what I like. Think of it, I can finish what I need to here and then we can get married. We can

166 · JODIE TOOHEY

just settle in without having the work of setting up house."

"How long?"

"A month should do it. I'm certain of it." She actually wasn't all that certain, but she hoped a month would buy her the time she needed.

William sighed. "Very well. I'll leave later this week."

"Oh, thank you!" Alice threw her arms around William's neck and he picked her up off her feet in his embrace.

"One month," he said, putting her down and looking into her eyes.

"One month," she said.

For two days, all Alice could think about was how she could find the evidence she needed to prove that Joseph killed Marty. The day before, Alice pretended she was down with her monthly pains. As soon as she knew Abigail was busy getting the children breakfast, she snuck into her room and found Joseph's diary where she remembered Abigail mentioning she'd had it hid. She read every page. It gave her plenty of reasons why he might've killed Marty, but it stopped before the tornado, so provided nothing proving he did. Knowing if she claimed pains a second day, she would be faced with a visit to the doctor, Alice listened to be sure everyone was downstairs and put the diary back where she found it. *Useless*, she thought as she tucked it back under Abigail's mattress.

She found the table stacked with piles of eggs, bacon, and toasted sliced bread. "Is it a holiday?" Alice asked, noticing the happiness glowing in Abigail's face.

Abigail laughed. "No, silly. I couldn't sleep because I'm so happy, so I guess I overdid breakfast."

Alice pulled out her chair out and suspiciously sat down. She examined the platters of food and chose an egg from the middle and a piece of bacon from the bottom.

As she reached for a piece of toast, Abigail said, "Is that still warm? I can reheat it for you if you'd like."

"No, it's alright," Alice said.

The children were already eating when Abigail sat down with her empty plate in front of her. She stretched both her arms out on the table, her palms up. "I have something to tell you all," she sang more than said, "Joseph and I are getting married!"

Alice dropped her fork, and a bit of egg fell onto the table with a splat. She picked it up with her thumb and index finger and dropped it back on her plate. She looked toward her sister.

"Isn't it wonderful? He asked me last night. And I said yes."

Alice leapt from her chair. It fell behind her with a bang. "But Marshall just died."

Samuel, David, and Josie halted their chatter. They looked at Abigail and Alice with wide eyes.

Abigail calmly picked up Alice's chair and pushed her into it by her shoulders. "Calm down and sit down," she said. When Alice sat back in her own chair and folded her hands in her lap,

Abigail said, "Marshall has been gone for over two years now, so it is certainly not improper for me to be remarrying."

"But what if he leaves you again?"

"Joseph is a changed man. He won't leave again. He promised, and I believe him. He was a boy then, but the war has made him a man." Abigail sighed. "I thought you'd be happy, Alice, to have someone to help with the farm and the chores to free you up for other *things*."

The way she emphasized "things," Alice wondered if she knew about William. It was possible; it seemed everyone in Camanche found out about things just as if they'd been there to witness them themselves. And so it was the same with the news of Joseph and Abigail's engagement. Realizing it would be useless to try to change Abigail's mind, Alice's immediately began racing, panicked she wouldn't be able to prove Joseph's guilt before he became her new brother-in-law. And Josie's new father.

CHAPTER THIRTEEN

Friday, September 8, 1865

The reaction to news of Abigail's impending marriage to Joseph was mixed. Some chittered about how she'd not waited long enough after her husband had died, but the ladies were fascinated with the romance of it all. Her old beau coming back into her life, unable to stay away. Though she usually avoided her, as soon as William left that morning to seek their new home, Alice went to see Deedra Mahoney, the person in town you told news to when you wanted it to spread as fast as possible. She found her sitting under a parasol in her yard, sipping lemonade, surely spiked with the highest quality white sugar.

"Miss Alice Sinkey," she said, waving her over. "It's so nice of you to pay me a visit. Won't you sit down and have some lemonade?" She turned toward her house, careful to keep the sun blocked from her pale face. "Mother!"

A woman, her hair pulled back into a tight bun and a splattered-upon apron hanging off her thin frame, appeared at the screen door. "Mother, won't you bring me a glass and some ice, so my dear friend, Alice, here can enjoy some lemonade?"

The woman scowled but didn't decline. A few moments later, she brought out a glass with a rough diamond pattern etched into the sides, already forming a thin film of condensation. She held it out to Deedra, who stared back at her.

Alice jumped up and took the glass from her. "Thank you, Mrs. Mahoney. It's been so long since I enjoyed lemonade." Alice poured the pale yellow liquid from the carafe into her glass.

Mrs. Mahoney smiled at Alice, saying, "You're welcome, dear." She glared at her daughter before returning to the house.

"So what brings you by on this hot day?" Deedra asked.

"A social visit. It seems like we haven't spoken in ages."

"You're absolutely right. How was your summer?"

Alice thought a moment about how to respond. "Eventful."

"So I hear. I've heard your sister is preparing to bring you another brother-in-law."

Heard? More like told. "Yes, her previous beau, Joseph Sund, decided after all of the time away in the war that he couldn't bear to be without her any longer."

"Oh, yes. We were so young back then, weren't we? It seems I recall my parents talking about how he was under suspicion for murdering that fellow during the tornado. What was that gent's name?"

"I don't remember." Alice tried to think of a way to steer the conversation where she wanted it to go. "But Abigail is getting married again."

"And what about your plans?"

Aha. "I've been thinking about that. With a husband for my sister back in the house, she should be able to resume her duties with the house and child rearing. Of course, I'll be around to help, especially with my brothers. But I have been thinking about settling down. Things didn't work out with my last beau. He up and moved back to Tennessee." Thankful William tended to be quiet with everyone but her, she tried her best to be coy, bowing and tilting her head. "You don't know of any good prospects, do you?"

Deedra laughed. "Me? No, not me. The only one I know of is Jason Macelroy." She set her lemonade on the side table, leaned toward Alice, and patted her knee. "But he's mine."

"Of course. You both are so well suited for each other."

"Thank you."

Alice drained the rest of her lemonade and felt the grittiness of the undissolved white sugar on her tongue. "I really must be going. Thank you for so much for the lemonade. It was delicious." She stood and held out her arms.

Deedra rose into them and hugged Alice back so lightly, it was more of a quick pat on the arms. "It was so nice of you to drop by. Please do come more often and not wait so long."

"I won't. Good afternoon."

Alice stopped by the store to pick up a few things and then stopped by Mrs. Alban's to gather Josie and her brothers so Abigail could complete her afternoon sewing unencumbered. By the time she returned to the post office before taking the children home, she already felt eyes on her back and heard abruptly cut-off conversations, sure they were already talking about how desperate she was for a man.

CHAPTER FOURTEEN

Thursday, September 14, 1865

Over the next few days, several suitors showed interest in her, but none of them felt right to Alice. None felt like the right person to help her with her cause until Mr. Robert Matthews came calling. Alice remembered Abigail mentioning that Mr. Matthews was a friend of Joseph's from before he left. She recalled Abigail talking about how peculiar it had been that he hadn't received a goodbye from Joseph or heard anything from him after he left, either. Alice had no time to spare.

"Mr. Matthews, it's so good to see you again," she told him the second time he stopped by the house.

"Please call me Robert."

"All right. Robert." She touched his arm. "Can you stay a while?"

"Perhaps for a few minutes."

Alice motioned to the chairs on the front porch. "Have a seat. Can I get you a glass of water?"

"No, thank you. I can't stay that long."

"I'll be right out." Josie was upstairs taking a nap, so Alice went through the house and out to the back where the boys were playing, their clothes covered in mud. "I'll be on the porch if you need me," she said. "I have a guest, so please behave back here and don't bother us unless it's important. And be quiet if you go in the house. Josie is sleeping."

The boys agreed, and Alice returned to Robert. She found him sitting in the far chair toward the porch's railing, sitting up straight, his right ankle resting on his left knee. He stood up and held out his hand. Alice took it and sat down in the chair next to him. When she was safely seated, he sat back down. "I'm surprised to see you. Happily."

Robert didn't respond. *What is he waiting for?*

"Were you stopping by to visit? Because that's fine. Or was there something particular you wanted?"

"They're having a dance at Brown's Brick Saturday evening and I wondered if I could be your escort. If you were going. Or if you weren't going, if you would."

"I'd heard about that. It sounds fun. I would need to check with my sister, but I'm sure she won't mind. I'd love to go with you."

Robert slapped his hands on his knees. "I'm so glad. I'd like to take you to dinner first, if I may. Would it be alright to come by at six to pick you up?"

"That sounds perfect," Alice said, standing. "I'll see you then."

After a moment, Robert followed Alice's lead. He kissed her palm before turning to leave. Alice heard him whistling all the way to his horse. *Yes, this one will do.*

On Saturday, Robert arrived right on time with his black carriage obviously recently washed, glinting brightly in the early evening sun. He took her to dinner. Alice found her pan-fried ribeye difficult to maneuver since she didn't enjoy the taste of fat, but the meat, when she pried a piece away, was salty and delicious, with a hint of smoke where it was cooked over an open fire. Robert told her he'd been saving up, so she could get anything she wanted. She ordered a glass of red wine because it was the only wine she'd ever tasted. She was grateful that neither the waitress nor Robert questioned the appropriateness of drinking it at her age. She sipped the wine, which tasted more bitter and dried her mouth out more than she remembered, but after a few drinks, her belly began to warm and she felt more at ease. Alice touched Robert whenever she got a chance. Her hand on his forearm, a brush of his fingers, and a few times, touching her leg against his as she switched crossing positions. He talked about his life before Camanche, and Alice jumped on the opening in the conversation.

"Why hasn't there yet been a Mrs. Matthews?" she asked.

Robert wiped his mouth with his napkin and returned it to his lap. "I suppose I just haven't come across the right young lady yet."

Alice batted her eyelashes at him. "And what would the right young lady look like?"

He grinned. *Why do men always fall for such outlandish things?*

"Let me think. I think she'd have beautiful golden hair that she wore gathered loosely over her shoulder." Alice pulled her hair around her head so it draped over the front of her left shoulder. Robert laughed and leaned toward her, resting his elbow on the table. Alice copied him. "And I think she'd have green eyes," he said with her lips so close to her face, she could smell the malted grain of beer on his breath.

"Oh, Mr. Matthews, you shouldn't lead a girl on like that."

He leaned back in his chair and took a gulp of his beer. "What makes you think I'm leading you on?"

Alice copied the charade when Robert asked her what a suitable husband would look like.

At the dance, Alice let Robert hold her tightly and bring her punch. The festivities ended at eleven and Alice counted on her family being fast asleep at home. After he helped her into the carriage and climbed in himself, Alice said, "It's been such a wonderful evening. I don't want it to end."

"It doesn't have to. We could take a ride."

"That sounds wonderful." He drove to a secluded spot along the river. Alice said, "I love how the moonlight makes a line across the water, don't you?"

"I do." He put his index finger on Alice's lower jaw and turned her face toward his. "I love even more how it makes your beautiful face glow."

Alice lowered her eyelids and thought of pulling away, but then she let his lips fall into hers. She let the wine take over as she opened her lips and let his tongue explore her mouth. When his hand started to slide from her neck down her shoulder, she pulled back and sank toward the opposite corner of the carriage.

"Alice, I'm sorry. You're just too beautiful."

"It's alright. I had to stop before I couldn't."

He took her hand in his and held it on the leather seat between then. "Let's get married," he said, "and then we wouldn't have to wait."

"We'd have to wait until our wedding night. And it's too late to get married right now."

"Of course." He turned and looked upriver before swinging his head back. "You mean you'll do it? You'll marry me?"

"Yes, I will," she said, plastering on her brightest smile.

"Tomorrow. We can go to the Justice of the Peace tomorrow."

Alice slid toward him and put her hands on his shoulders, pulling him to face her squarely. "I want to. I really do, but I need to settle some things first. And you can help me."

"Settle what things? How can I help you?"

"I'll tell you what you need to know as we go along. But you'll do it?"

"After that you'll marry me?"

"Yes." Alice felt horrible for leading Robert on, but she couldn't think of another way to find out the truth.

CHAPTER FIFTEEN

Monday, September 18, 1865

Though she had heard Lucy was back at school, Alice waited to see her go into the building to make sure before she went to pay her mother a visit. She knocked on the door and saw Pamela smiling sweetly until her eyes met Alice's and her face fell.

She opened the door a crack. "Lucy's at school."

"I know. I came by to see you. I wanted to apologize for the trouble my sister caused."

Pamela's face softened, and she let Alice in. "Have a seat," she said, pointing to an elegant settee in the parlor. "Can I get you anything to drink?"

"No, thank you. I know you're busy and I don't want to trouble you for long. I wanted to apologize for my sister getting involved with the whole business with …" Pamela covered her eyes with her outstretched hand. "Well, you know. Anyway, it wasn't her place."

Pamela nodded her head and whispered, "Thank you," not indicating any degree of forgiveness.

"You've heard that she's planning to marry Joseph Sund?"

"I did." Pamela's face visibly paled.

"I'm very worried."

Pamela lowered her eyes to her lap. "Oh?"

"I'm worried because I believe Joseph may have been the one who killed Mr. Cranson." Pamela picked at her fingernails. "I heard that you thought you saw Joseph there when Mr. Cranson was murdered." More silence. "Please, Mrs. Mackenrow. I know you are not fond of my sister, and I understand, but I'm looking out for my brothers and niece. If a murderer is moving in with them, I need to know."

Pamela opened her mouth but snapped it shut.

"You don't have to say anything. If it was Joseph who you saw there, just nod your head. Was Joseph the person you thought you saw?"

Pamela nodded.

"Thank you," Alice replied, standing. "I'd appreciate it if you didn't mention my visit to Lucy. She seems to think my family and I have caused enough trouble already." A lump formed in her throat. "But please know I miss and love her. And if she ever needs anything, I'm here to help her." She swallowed and held her breath, composing herself. Pamela didn't look up, so Alice lightly touched her shoulder before letting herself out.

She stalled until the lunch bell, sitting by the river searching her mind for what else she could do. When it rang, she found Robert eating. As she approached, she saw that he put his fingers in his mouth with each bite and then wiped them on his shirt. Alice's stomach turned, but she found her best smile.

Robert lit up when he saw her. "Alice! What a nice surprise." He thrust his hand toward her, but she pretended not to notice and buried her hands in her skirts.

"I'm sorry to bother you," she said.

"It's no bother. It's good to see you. Why don't we go over here to talk?" He put his hand on her back and she tried to walk faster to race ahead as Robert's lunchmates snickered. When they got far enough away that she could no longer hear the snickers, Alice stopped and turned to Robert.

"Have you spoken with Joseph?"

"Yes. We had a few drinks last night to celebrate his engagement."

"What did he say? What does he know about Marty's murder?"

He hesitated, so Alice placed her hands on his upper arm and leaned into him. She stretched to her toes and whispered in his ear, "I can't *think* of marriage until I know my family's safe." She lowered herself to her heels and pleaded at him with her eyes.

Robert sighed like he'd been holding his breath since she'd arrived. "He said he did it." Alice backed away. "But he had so much to drink, I don't know if he really knew what he was saying."

"That's all I need to know," she said, leaving him standing, looking bewildered.

Alice barged into the stationhouse. "I know who did it!" she told the officer at the first desk she saw.

"Calm down, Miss. You know who did what?"

She bent over and put her hands on her knees, trying to catch her breath after running all the way there. "I know … who killed … Marty Cranson."

"Come on back here." The officer led her into a room off the main area of the police station. "Have a seat," he said, pointing to a chair on the

190 · JODIE TOOHEY

opposite side of a desk. He walked around and sat in the chair on the other side. He leaned back so far Alice thought he might topple to the floor. "Tell me what you mean, that you know who killed Marty Cranson."

"It was Joseph Sund."

"That's a serious claim, Miss …?"

"Sinkey."

"Miss Sinkey, do you have any evidence to support this serious claim you make?"

"Mrs. Pamela Mackenrow told me that she remembered seeing him there the night Marty was shot, just before she passed out."

The officer let his chair fall back to the floor. It banged on the wooden planks and he leaned forward, resting his elbows on the desk's top. "Miss Sinkey, I'm afraid there's nothing we can do."

"But she said he was there. Who else could've done it? It was Joseph's gun. She said you already knew that."

"We know that Mrs. Mackenrow says she recalled Joseph there immediately before Mr. Cranson was shot. However, Mrs. Mackenrow also previously went on record saying that she was the one who shot the man. We cannot rely on her words to arrest someone. It was one thing when it was just herself she was locking up. We can't lock someone else up based on someone words, especially if those words have already been found to come from someone as unreliable as Mrs. Mackenrow."

Alice shook her head. "So that's it?"

"I'm afraid so."

"But Joseph is my sister's beau. They're planning to get married. I can't rely on him leaving her again. I can't take the chance of letting him marry my sister. Her words are enough to make me not want him to live with in the same house as my little brothers or my niece. Or me."

"Then we need convincing physical evidence. You find that information and bring it to me, then we can do something. I'm afraid that's all I can offer you."

Shaking with fear, anger, and futility, Alice stood up. "What would you do if you were me?"

"It's best you leave detective work up the professionals. Don't do anything directly yourself. If you hear of anything, tell me and let me handle it."

Like you've handled it this far?

"Alright, Miss Sinkey?"

"Yes."

CHAPTER SIXTEEN

Tuesday, September 19, 1865

On Tuesday, Alice met Robert at Cutler's. He told her about how he found Joseph after dropping her off and convinced him to have more drinks with him to celebrate his upcoming nuptials. Robert put his arms around Alice's shoulders.

"What did he say?" Alice asked.

"He said he heard that Pamela confessed to murdering Marty and was sent to the asylum. Knowing there would be no suspicion cast on him and because he still cared so much for Abigail, when he was mustered out of the war, he came back.

"He met Marshall at the battle of Vicksburg. When they talked about back home and Marshall mentioned his wife, Abigail, her twin brothers and sister in Camanche, Iowa, he realized who Marshall was. He said he wasn't exactly sure why but he had a hunch that he shouldn't connect himself to Camanche. Since he went by Joe during the war, he was just careful to never mention his last name. He put off like he'd lived in Ohio his entire life.

"During the battle, I guess he got confused. He said he got in a fist fight with Marshall. He hit Marshall on the head with the butt of his gun. Blood trickled down his temple and he thought he'd killed him. He said he worried that he'd somehow be connected to Camanche, Abigail, and Marshall and they'd think he'd killed Marshall intentionally. I remember I was shocked when he said that he'd already thought about killing him on account of pure jealousy over his moving in on Abigail. He said he noticed someone else nearby who looked like Marshall who had been shot in the head, so he took whatever he could find identifying Marshall so he could switch it the identification of the man who had been shot. But before he had a chance, he heard someone coming so he dropped everything and ran."

Alice sat up straight. "That means that Marshall might not be dead. He could be alive somewhere. I have to find him." She got up and started to run toward home, but turned around to find a shocked look on Robert's face. She ran back and kissed him on the lips. This time it was sincere and not just part of her game.

The first chance she had, she snuck to the Clinton post office on horseback. They gave her addresses to every hospital where soldiers were sent. She wrote a letter to each one of them, with a note enclosed addressed to Marshall in case he was there:

Dear Marshall,

I hope this correspondence finds you. I have been searching for you in all of the hospitals I could find. We were informed on July 16, 1863, that you had been killed at the battle of Vicksburg, but I've since uncovered the information that you may still be living. My sister – your wife

– needs you. Please return home at once, or if you are unable, please reply at your first chance.

Lovingly, your sister-in-law,

Alice Sinkey

CHAPTER SEVENTEEN

Monday, October 2, 1865

The days with no response turned into weeks as Alice eagerly waited for the mail and watched for Marshall's familiar frame to approach. Finally, a letter arrived with the return address at the Bishop Hill Colony Hospital. Inside, the letter read:

Dear Miss Sinkey,

I'm sorry that I can neither refute or affirm that I am the Marshall Stevenson you seek. I was wounded at the battle of Vicksburg with a severe blow to my head. Since that time, I've been laid up in the hospital unable to remember anything prior to when I woke from my unconsciousness. I eventually remembered my name, but that is all.

I may very well be your brother-in-law and am very interested in the information that I may have a family. My doctors have told me that it may only take something or someone from my past to trigger the return of all my memories, but I'm unable to travel and won't until I can recover completely. I'd be most appreciative of any help you can provide in allowing me to remember whether or not I am the person who is the subject of your search.

Gratefully yours,

Marshall Stevenson

Alice scribbled a return note that she would come to see him as soon as she was able, and immediately crafted her plan to make the trip. She would leave the next morning before first light, leaving a note for Abigail explaining that there was something she had to do, not to worry, and she'd be back as soon as possible. After the house was quiet and everyone was asleep that night, she packed a bag with an extra dress, underclothes, all the cash she could find, and all the family photos she could find with recent likenesses of

Abigail, the twins, Josie, and especially the one from the wedding with Marshall.

*****

She went directly to the hospital, let off in front of the door into an early, drizzly gray afternoon. She lugged her bag to the front desk and set it down at her feet.

"May I help you?"

"Yes, please. I'm here to see Marshall Stevenson."

"Are you family?"

"I'm his sister-in-law, Alice Sinkey."

"Very well. He's upstairs, fourth bed in."

"Thank you."

She stepped into a long room with several beds lined up in front of a parade of open windows, designed to let in bright sunlight and fresh air on clearer days. She held her bag in both hands in front of her, took a deep breath, and walked in. She counted the beds, one, two, three,

four. The man in the bed lay with his face pointing away from her, his head wrapped in a white
gauze bandage. She walked between his bed and
bed number three. He didn't move his body, but
just his head turned to look at her. He looked different, but she recognized him immediately as
Marshall.

"It's really you," she said. "He was right.
You are alive."

Marshall pushed his fists into the bed,
grunted himself to a seated position, and slid
back so he was leaning against the scrolled iron
headboard.

"Do I know you?" he asked.

"It's me, Alice. Did you get my letter saying I was coming to see you?"

He rubbed his eyes and took an envelope
from the small table beside his bed. "Yes, I did.
I'm sorry. I must still be half asleep." He looked
her up and down, squinting, obviously trying to
get his brain to connect the image in front of him
to his past. "You're my sister-in-law?"

Alice nodded her head. "You married my sister, Abigail Sinkey, before you left for the war. My brothers, Samuel and David, are twins. They are eight years old now, five when you left. And …" She trailed off, not knowing how he'd feel when he heard about the last member of the family.

Marshall swung his legs off the side of the bed. "Do I … Do I have children?"

Alice pulled up the chair next to her, wedged between Marshall's bed and the bedside table of bed number three. She held her bag so it rested on top of her feet. "One. A daughter. Her name is Josephine, after my mother. We call her Josie, like my mother's friends and my father used to call her."

"How old is she?"

"Two. Almost three."

"My military papers say I was mustered in August 1862. When is her birthday?"

"You left before she was born. It was January 20, 1863."

"Do you have a photograph?"

"I do. I brought photographs." Alice unbuttoned her bag and pulled out the scrapbook in which she'd affixed the pictures. She flipped through until she found the most recent one of Josie and passed the book to him, pointing at it. "Here. This is Josie."

Marshall brought the book toward his face, scrutinizing the likeness. "She's beautiful." He looked around the room. "Do you have a mirror?"

"She has your nose and eyes," Alice said.

"I thought so." He put the book down on his lap and closed his eyes. Alice saw a tear slip down his cheek.

"I'm sorry. I didn't mean to …"

"No, it's alright. This is obviously my little girl. I know I never met her, but I must've seen her picture before. I must've written her letters. I just wish I could remember. Or at least remember her mother. My wife."

Alice reached over, flipping the pages to the one taken the day of their wedding. "Here she is," she said pointing at Abigail's wedding dress. "This was the day you were married."

Marshall pulled his legs up, slipping them under his covers so he was again sitting with his back against the headboard. He dropped his head into his hands and wept. Alice's heart broke for him, and for a moment, before remembering the urgent reason she was there, she felt sorry that she'd come to him at all. She swallowed her own tears and said, "Maybe you should get some rest. I saw a hotel on my way. I'll get a room there and come back in the morning. I'll leave the photos here so you can look through them when you're ready."

He didn't say anything but nodded his head in agreement. Alice squeezed his hand before leaving.

Not knowing an appropriate time to return the next morning, Alice lingered over an egg and three cups of coffee in the hotel's dining room, sipping them to make the time and her money last longer. She got many quizzical looks thrown her way, but only one person spoke to her, an older woman, her gray hair twisted in a bun.

"I'm sorry, Miss," she said. "But I can't help but notice you seem to be awfully young to be away from home without your parents."

Alice laughed. "Don't worry. I get this all the time. I have a very young-looking face. I know it's unusual, but I assure you, I'm grown at eighteen and don't need my parents to escort me."

"I see."

"I'm here visiting my brother-in-law at the hospital. He was injured in the war." At least that part was true.

"Is he one of the Swede boys?" The confusion must've shown on Alice's face. The woman continued, "Those poor boys. They were late arriving at Fort Donnellson and Shiloh, and their rifles malfunctioned. They were in Company D of the 57th Illinois."

"My brother-in-law was in the Iowa 20th."

The woman beamed. "You must be so proud. I always liked it when Lincoln referred to the 'Westerners' saving the day at Pittsburgh Landing or Shiloh. 'Westerners' – from Iowa. That's just barely west if you ask me. Was your fella at Fort Donnellson or Shiloh?"

"I don't know. He was kill … injured at Vicksburg."

Her face fell, and the old woman laid her dry, wrinkled hand on top of Alice's, clutched to her coffee cup handle. Her other hand, she laid flat on her chest. "I'm so sorry, dear. Please give your brother-in-law my best. I'll pray for him."

"Thank you," Alice said, patting the old woman's hand with her free hand. As the woman walked away, Alice looked at the clock on the hotel restaurant's wall. There were two minutes until ten o'clock, so Alice left enough money on the table to pay her bill and headed to the hospital.

When she arrived, she found Marshall fully dressed, his bed made neatly. He was sitting on the edge, fidgeting his fingers. His head was still wrapped, but his eyes were brighter. "You're finally here. I've been waiting for you for hours."

"I wasn't sure what time I should come," she said. "I didn't want to interrupt your rest."

He waved her over to him. "Come here. Sit down."

Alice angled the chair next to his bed so she could face him better and sat. He opened the photo book she had left and laid it in her lap. He pointed to the wedding photograph.

"The doctors were right. That one's Samuel," he said. "We went swimming in the river once and he got his foot caught on something in the river. I had to pull him out. Your sister – my wife – was so scared and she was angry at first."

Alice looked up at him. He remembered! A wide smile spread across her face and she fought the urge to throw her arms around his neck.

"And David. He's the more serious of the two."

"That's right!"

"I remember there was someone else important to the wedding, too. We went to her house after the ceremony where she had the most delicious cakes."

"Mrs. Alban. Yes. She prepared them for us during the ceremony and we went to her house afterwards. She has been such a help to us since our parents died."

The smile fell from Marshall's face. "I'm sorry. I remember that, too. Your parents died in that terrible tornado, the one that brought me to Abigail and your family."

Alice swallowed the saliva funneling into her throat and coughed to clear it completely. "Abigail needs you."

"I know. I'm her husband. She must be terribly worried."

Alice squirmed. She actually didn't know how Abigail would react to the news that she couldn't marry Joseph because she was still married to Marshall.

"I'll go to her as soon as I'm able," Marshall said. "Please tell her I love her. Yes, I remember that, too. Tell her now that I remember, and since she knows for sure it was me here, tell her to come see me. And bring my daughter. Bring my Josie."

Alice sucked in a deep breath. "You don't understand. Abigail doesn't know I'm here."

"I understand. You didn't want to get her hopes up until you were sure."

"Not exactly. Abigail's in trouble. Do you remember Joseph Sund?"

Marshall was silent for a minute. "I think I do remember. I had thought Abigail was mad because she thought this Joseph had murdered the man who was killed during the tornado, but it was a gunshot, not the storm. But Abigail found out that Pamela woman in town had done it. I was on my way out of town when she caught up to me and told me."

"She wasn't mad and Pamela didn't do it. At the asylum where they sent her, she remembered she didn't do it, and she remembered seeing Joseph there."

"Have the police found this Joseph yet?"

"They aren't looking for him. They said her words were not enough evidence to arrest him."

"I don't understand. What does this have to do with Abigail and me?"

"Joseph is back in Camanche, Marshall. He's won Abigail back and they are preparing to get married. I've been trying to find real evidence that Joseph killed Marty, but I haven't been able to yet. Abigail needs to know that she can't marry Joseph because she's still married to you. I need you to come home with me right away." She purposely left out her knowledge of Marshall's and Joseph's meeting at Vicksburg; she was afraid it would be too much for Marshall to handle.

Marshall felt his head. "I have been feeling much better and the doctor just told me I would be discharged within a few days." He looked around the room. "Let's go. My bag is under the bed."

Alice reached under the bed, pulled it out, and plopped it on top of the covers. It was empty and looked like a deflated pig bladder after the kids had batted it around all afternoon on butchering day. Marshall walked around his bed to the nightstand. He grabbed the few items in its drawer, stuffed them in the bag, and buttoned it up. He grabbed Alice's elbow. "Come on, let's go."

The patients in the beds next to Marshall stirred in response to all the commotion. They sat up and looked at him. As they walked out, the one next to the door, his wrapped leg stump suspended in the air, pointed to them and hollered toward the end of the room. As they reached the elevator, they heard a nurse behind them.

"Wait. Where are you going? You can't leave. The doctor needs to discharge you."

She got to within five feet of them when the elevator doors closed. They stopped by the hotel to grab Alice's things and went straight to the train station.

CHAPTER EIGHTEEN

Saturday, October 7, 1865

The stage arrived just as the sun was reaching its highest point, nearly eliminating any shadows. The driver took their bags from the coach's top and handed them to Alice and Marshall, who took them both. Alice grabbed hers away from him.

"I think you should take it easy," she said. "Remember you left the hospital earlier than you were supposed to."

Marshall nodded and started walking toward the house.

"Wait!" Alice said. "We need to see someone first."

"I thought you said Abigail needed me right away?"

"I had someone looking into things while I was away. We need to find out if he learned anything important. I sent him a message telling him when we'd arrive and told him to meet us here." Alice looked around the stagecoach as it pulled away and saw Robert running toward them. His eyes were flashing, his excitement unmistakable.

"I just got your message," he said, bending over, holding his torso up with his hands on his knees, trying to catch his breath. He stood back up, clutching his middle and smiling. "He did it. He confessed. Joseph told me that he killed Marty Cranson. Now we can get married." He held his arms out toward Alice. Just as his hands reached her waist, she turned toward Marshall and threw her arms around his neck.

"When?" she asked. "Do the police have him?"

"The police?"

"Yes. Wasn't that enough evidence for the police to arrest him?"

"I didn't go to the police."

Abigail planted her hands on her hips and glared at Robert.

"I thought you wanted to know for yourself. I didn't know you were trying to get Joseph arrested," Robert said.

"Of course I want him arrested. He killed a man. Where is he now?"

A tint of grey seemed to fall over Robert's face. "I just saw him. He was on his way to your place. He said he was going to try to convince Abigail to marry him today."

Alice looked at Marshall. His face was red with fury. He stomped off.

She called after him, "Marshall, wait. She has the children. She wouldn't leave the children. And she wouldn't take them with her to get married."

She heard Robert panting behind her as she tried to catch up with Marshall. "He said the children were in playing with the Wilkes children today, so it would be the perfect time."

Alice ran faster, but she couldn't catch up with Marshall. By the time she reached home, choking from trying to breathe and her heart pounding, he was already there. She shoved the door open and saw Marshall on top of Joseph, who was pinned to the ground with Marshall's forearm pushing down on his throat. Abigail clung to the floor, half sitting and half lying down, her face showing her obvious shock.

"Marshall, wait!" Alice called.

Marshall eased his forearm up from Joseph's throat, "Tell me, *Joe*! Tell me the truth!"

Joseph's eyes squinted, and his face screwed up tight. "All right," he said. "I did it. I killed Marty. I had to." Joseph sobbed like a baby. Marshall let go; he sat up and scooted back toward the wall. Abigail's hands splayed over her wide open mouth. Marshall inched closer to him.

"What happened? Tell me everything."

"It was the night of the tornado." Joseph stood and turned toward Abigail. "I felt so bad about leaving that I went on a spree Saturday night and slept it off most of the day Sunday.

When I woke up, I went to the river where the guys were fishing to tell them goodbye. After that, I was going to grab my things, come here to tell Abigail goodbye, and be on my way to Ohio." He made a move toward Abigail, but Marshall put his open palm on the middle of Joseph's chest.

"Stay there," Marshall said. "Keep going."

Joseph stepped back and put his hands in the air. "All right. As I was getting my things, I heard a commotion down the hall, so I went to see what it was. I heard it again and realized it was coming from behind Marty's door. I didn't notice until then that it had gotten so dark, and then I heard this horrible roar. The next thing I knew, the windows blew in. Glass flew everywhere and something, to this day I don't know what it was, but something struck Pamela. She fell to the floor and I saw my gun. It fell to the floor and bounced on the wood. Marty lunged for it, but I grabbed it first. He grabbed for my hand and I pulled the trigger. I didn't even realize I'd done it. I heard the bang from the shot and saw

218 · JODIE TOOHEY

Marty slump to the floor before I realized I'd pulled the trigger."

Joseph buried his head in his hands. "I didn't know what to do. I thought that Pamela was dead, too, so I put the gun back on the floor where it landed when Pamela dropped it, or it was knocked out of her hand by whatever hit her. And then I left as fast as I could."

Alice put her arms around Abigail's shoulders and pulled her sister toward her.

"The sounds of all of the people hurting and injured as I left haunted me for months. But I couldn't think. I didn't know what else to do."

Alice started to feel sorry for Joseph.

"If it was an accident, you could've went to the police," Marshall said. "You could've stuck around to see if Pamela was alive. You could've not been a coward and stuck around to see if the person you claimed you loved and her family were alright after the storm. But you didn't."

Joseph's body visibly stiffened and he reached his hand behind his back. Before Alice knew what was happening, she saw the sunlight coming in through the window flash off a gun in Joseph's hand. He lunged toward both girls, but Abigail slipped away. He grabbed Alice, wedging her head in his bent left arm while he held the gun to her head with his right hand. "Stay back!"

Marshall held his hands out and stepped toward Joseph and Alice. "You've never killed anyone on purpose. Let her go."

Alice heard a click in her right ear. Abigail screamed, "No!" and jumped in front of Marshall.

Joseph pulled Alice backward toward the door. She tripped and he adjusted his grip on her, sliding his arm down to her stomach and carrying her out like a sack of potatoes as he pointed the gun at Marshall and Abigail, back and forth until they got out the door. He grabbed a rope, tied it around Alice's hands, and threw her up onto the horse. He pointed the gun at her with one hand while he used the other to order Alice to grab the horn and tie her hands to it with the rope. He jumped on the horse behind her and kicked its flanks, pointing it southwest.

CHAPTER NINETEEN

Monday, October 9, 1865

Joseph followed the river until it started to turn south, and then they left it getting further and further behind them. Alice, lethargic with exhaustion and hunger, asked, "Where are you taking me?"

"I'll know when we get there. I've never been this way before, so I figure that would be the least likely direction they'd look."

"What are you going to do when we get there?"

Joseph didn't answer. Alice started to cry.

"What's the matter? Is the rope hurting you?"

"I'm hungry, and I need to use the privy."

Joseph headed toward a stand of trees in the distance. As they got closer, Alice saw they were apple trees. He tied the horse to one of them and helped Alice down. He untied her hands and pointed the gun at her from around the other side of the tree while she did her business, trying not to make a mess of her clothes. When she was done, he motioned her to sit on the ground in front of a different tree.

"Wait here. I'll pick some apples," he said.

He kept the gun pointed at her; she could see him watching her out of the corner of his eyes. He tried to pull the apples with his other arm, but they were too high, so with a determined look on his face, he tucked his gun into his waistband and climbed up the tree. Alice took her opportunity. She scrambled to her feet. She only got a few steps before she heard Joseph yell, "Get back here!" from behind her and he tackled her to the ground. Alice kicked and flailed, but he managed to get her back to the tree where he used the rope to tie her to it by her waist.

Joseph let Alice have two apples, fed a few to the horse, and stuffed as many as would fit into the horse's saddlebags. The eastern sky was darkening and the sun started to sink, creating a brilliant yellow in the west.

"We'll spend the night here," Joseph said, "and start again at first light." He started a fire and put the blanket underneath the horse's saddle over Alice, where she still sat leaning against the tree, tied to it by her waist. Joseph lay in front of her, between her and the fire, his left arm clutching her ankle and his right arm clutching his gun, rested on his belly, pointed toward Alice. She was too terrified to move.

CHAPTER TWENTY

Tuesday, October 10, 1865

Alice awoke just as the sky was starting to lighten into dawn. She tried to scoot herself around the tree, leaving the rope in place so she could get to the other side and untie it, but she only got a few inches when Joseph stirred. He let her eat two more apples, snuffed out the embers still left from the fire, and put her back on the horse, her hands tied.

As they rode, Alice noticed darkening clouds approaching from the west. Lightning flashed around them and the thunder reached their ears immediately.

"Can't we stop?" Alice asked, cowering herself into the horse as much as she could.

Joseph jumped from the saddle, pulling the horse, now hesitant and scared, to coax it on. "Do you see any place for us to go?"

Alice scanned the horizon. "No," she said feebly.

Rain drops as big as river pebbles fell on them. Alice tucked her chin into her chest to try to restrict the sting to where her hair and clothes could protect her somewhat. She got soaked as if she'd swum across the river in her clothes, and as the sun reappeared and dried her, sneezes jolted her and her head began to fill.

After a day and a half of hard travel, they'd arrived into Kansas. He stopped to rest next to a creek. "We should be coming up to a town soon," he said, handing her the last apple. "I've seen maps of this area before and seem to remember a town called Manhattan."

"What are we going to do when we get there?" Alice asked. She breathed through half of her nose and pulled the horse blanket Joseph had allowed her to use tighter around her shoulders.

"I don't know. Let me think."

As Joseph dozed, Alice tried to think of a way to escape, but she couldn't. Joseph had gotten smarter and tied a knot around her waist before fastening it to the tree, so if she tried to maneuver, the knot around the tree would always be to her back where she couldn't reach it. She felt so weak from sickness, she wasn't sure how far she could get if she could get loose. Alice closed her eyes and fell asleep. She awoke to a strange throaty rumbling. She looked over and saw Joseph crying.

"What is it?" she asked.

"I just don't know what to do," he said. "What have I done?"

Alice thought this might be her chance, so she sniffed and mustered up her sweetest voice. "You haven't done anything all that bad. Why don't we go back? We're out of food and we have no money to buy any, or to pay for a place to stay when we get to this Manhattan, and we're not even sure how far it is. We can go back the same way and get some more apples. You haven't hurt me. I'll tell them so."

228 · JODIE TOOHEY

"But I killed Marty. They'll hang me."

"Maybe not. Marty did so many bad things to you. You can tell them that. Abigail still has your diary. You can show that to the judge. When you shot him, he was attacking you and you said yourself you didn't mean to pull the trigger. That has to help you."

Joseph shook his head. "But what about Marshall?" He sighed loudly. "I used to be a good person, Alice. What happened to me?"

Alice strained against the rope around her waist to rest her hand gently on Joseph's back. "I don't know. You were desperate. Maybe they'll take that into account. What alternative do we have? You love Abigail, don't you?"

"Yes."

"And you know she loves me?"

"Yes."

"Think of how grateful she'll be to you when you bring me back so I can see a doctor. No matter what happens, you'll have made her so happy doing that."

"Perhaps you're right."

"I am right. Eventually, they will find us and you'll likely be punished worse for stealing me away. That's if we don't die from starvation or exposure first."

Joseph didn't say anything, just untied Alice from the tree and put the rope in a saddlebag. He climbed onto the horse and held his hand out to her. She took it and hoisted herself to sit behind Joseph in the saddle. She tucked her skirts around her legs, put her arms around Joseph, leaned into him, breathed a sigh of relief, and fell asleep.

CHAPTER TWENTY-ONE

Tuesday, October 17, 1865

When Joseph and Alice returned to Camanche, they went straight to the police station. They walked in and saw that Marshall and Abigail were there. As soon as Alice's eyes met Abigail's, Abigail jumped up and hugged her sister. Marshall lunged toward Joseph, but one of the officers stopped him.

"It's alright," Alice said. "I'm fine. Everything is fine. Joseph treated me well. He came back to turn himself in."

Joseph held his wrists together, and an officer wrapped handcuffs around them. Marshall smoothed his shirt over his chest as the officer let him go.

A sense of safety had just begun to wash over Alice in her sister's arms when she heard a bang behind her. She turned to see Pamela, waving an axe.

"Joseph Sund!" she said. They all backed away, the officers alternating pointing their weapons at Pamela and Joseph, leaving him standing in the middle of the room. Pamela lunged toward him, but James burst through the door just in time to wrap his arms around her from behind, sending the axe clanging to the floor.

Joseph cried. "I'm sorry. I shot Marty. But it was an accident. He lunged for me as the tornado hit and I accidentally pulled the trigger. At Vicksburg, I got confused and knocked Marshall out." He looked at the floor. "I thought I'd killed him. I panicked and ran." He turned toward Abigail. "I never meant to hurt you. I never stopped loving you. I'm just a coward who ran when he didn't know what to do."

Abigail pulled Alice's head into her chest. Marshall put his arms around them both.

Marshall, Abigail, and Alice returned home after collecting the twins and Josie from Mrs. Alban, who'd stepped in to watch them while Alice was away and Marshall and Abigail searched for her, returning after a day to see if Joseph had come back with her. Alice didn't eat, but fell straight into bed without putting on her nightclothes the moment she entered her bedroom.

When she awoke the next morning, the sun was high in the sky. It was quiet when she went downstairs. She looked out the front door to see Samuel, David, and Josie playing horses in the dirt. Marshall and Abigail sat on the steps, their sides touching. Alice saw them smiling, leaning their heads toward each other, talking in low, happy tones.

"Ahem." Alice tried to get their attention. They turned to her at the same time. Marshall slid away from Abigail.

"Come sit with us," he said.

Alice took a place between her sister and brother-in-law. They both put their arms around her shoulders, overlapping and feeling heavy.

"Did you sleep well?" Abigail asked.

Alice nodded her head, squinting at her brothers and niece playing in front of her. She bowed her head toward them. "What do they know about everything that happened?"

Abigail laughed. "They've hardly noticed anything at all happened. To be so young and so resilient!"

Marshall said, "The boys don't remember me, and of course, Josie never knew me, but when we explained to them that I was Josie's father and would be staying from now on, they just smiled and returned to their supper."

"Did they ask about Joseph?" Alice asked.

"David did. We told him he was just here visiting and had to go away now."

Abigail said, "They were more concerned about you and when you were coming back. I just told them you had to go on a little trip and would be back as soon as you could. After a day, they said they missed you and asked if you were coming home, but I didn't know, so I kept telling them soon. You saw how happy they were when they saw you at Mrs. Alban's."

Alice's heart filled as she watched them. The boys were so gentle with Josie, giving her their horses and showing her how to make them gallop.

"Now the question to answer is," Abigail said, "how long are you going to stay?"

"What do you mean?"

"When you left to find Marshall, I was sick with worry, trying to figure out where you'd gone and hoping you'd be safe. I found your diary and read about William. It's been almost a month since he left. Will you leave with him right away?"

"I don't think I'll be going anywhere." Alice smiled. "Somehow since Marshall is back and everything can get back to normal, the idea of cooking and cleaning for a husband doesn't sound so appealing. I think I'll stay here, relax, and maybe become a teacher for a while before I settle down."

CHAPTER TWENTY-TWO

Saturday, October 28, 1865

Alice had not reached out to William since he went away. He'd written to her twice, once to tell her he made it to Tennessee, and the other time to tell her how much he missed her, couldn't wait for them to be together, and that he'd found a beautiful home for them to live in. According to his letter, he would be back any day. Alice tried to think of what she would say when she finally saw him. Having watched Joseph and Abigail as well as Marshall and Abigail together, she'd realized that though she cared for William, there was no passion, nor mutual respect and companionship that could make a good marriage. She sat on the porch reading, something she'd gotten used to quickly as Marshall found a job, started working the farm, and Abigail resumed her duties of being mother and wife.

She was so engrossed in the story she read that she didn't notice William's carriage approaching from town. She didn't notice until she heard his horse whinny as he tied it up. He stepped down and Alice stood and laid her book face down on her chair. She was happy to see him, but there were no electric jolts or warm feelings in her middle. Only regret at what she knew she had to tell him.

Alice stepped off the porch steps. "William, you're back."

He rushed toward her, lifted her in his arms, and twirled in a circle. Alice stiffened and he set her on her feet. "What is it?" he asked.

"How was your trip?"

"I ran into a bit of rain about half way here in Illinois, but it was smooth other than that. How have you been? Did you … resolve what you needed to?"

"Yes. All is well." She thought about telling him the whole story, but she didn't have the energy. She crossed her arms in front of her chest.

"You're not coming back with me, are you?"

Alice looked up at him, swallowed, and shook her head. "No."

"May I ask why?"

"Our ages. You're much too much older than me."

"Ten years are not so many years. I know lots of couples who are more years apart in age."

"I haven't been completely honest with you. I'm not 18. I'm 15."

William slapped his hat against his leg and returned it to his head.

"I'm sorry. I really did like you. I've changed. I was looking for something," Alice said.

"Did you find it?"

"I don't know if I found or if I realized I didn't need it anymore. Maybe I never needed it. I just thought I did." Alice rubbed the three middle fingers on her right hand into her forehead. "That doesn't make any sense, does it?"

William stepped toward her and put his arm on her shoulder. "Actually, it does make sense. You've been through so much, it's understandable that you'd get confused about some things."

"Do you forgive me?"

He pulled her toward her and hugged her like she was an old friend. "Of course I forgive you." He pushed her away and stood, keeping her outstretched hand clasped in his. "I wish you the best, Alice." He let her hand go, untied his horse, and got back in the carriage, saying, "Give my best to your family," before riding away.

William was barely out of sight when Alice saw a familiar head of red hair approaching from town. She sat on the front step and waited. So many feelings rushed through her as she studied Lucy's face. She knew Lucy no longer had anything to be angry with her about, but she was nervous anyway. As she got closer, though, all Alice could see in Lucy's face was love, forgiveness, and regret.

The girls didn't have to say anything to each other. When they got close enough to see the tears in each other's eyes, they ran into each other's arms, the past melting away to leave them best friends again.

SELECTED BIBLIOGRAPHY

Bengston, M.L., Graham, R. & Halsrud, D., Editors. (1986). *Camanche, Iowa Charter City History Book*.

Bennett, W. (2010). *The American Patriot's Almanac*. Thomas Nelson.

Berry, V. & Hecker, C. (1997). *Roots and Recipes: Six Generations of Heartland Cookery*. Pelican Publishing Company, Inc.: Gretna, Louisiana.

Bogue, A.G. (1994). *From Prairie to Corn Belt: Farming on the Illinois and Iowa Prairies in the Nineteenth Century, 2nd ed*. Iowa State University Press: Ames, Iowa.

Bowbeer, A., Editor. (1976). *History of Clinton County Iowa*. Clinton County Historical Society: Clinton, Iowa.

Child, L.M. (1932) *The American Frugal Housewife*.

Child, L.M. (1834). *The Girl's Own Book.* Carter, Hendee and Babcock. Reprinted by Applewood Books.

Child, L.M. (1831). *The Mother's Book, 2nd ed.* Carter and Hendee. Reprinted by Applewood Books.

Clinton County Historical Society. (2003). *Images of America: Clinton Iowa.* Arcadia Publishing: Chicago.

Clinton County Historical Society. (2004). *Images of America: Clinton Iowa.* Arcadia Publishing: Chicago.

Clinton Herald. (Various Dates). Miscellaneous articles and advertisements from Microfilm.

Clinton Herald. (2004). *Clinton Once Upon a Time Sesquicentennial Edition from 1855-2005, Volume I.* Newspaper Holding, Inc.

Clinton Herald. (2005). *Clinton Once Upon a Time Sesquicentennial Edition from 1855-2005,* Volume II. Newspaper Holding, Inc.

Erickson, M. & Long, K. (1983). *Clinton: A Pictorial History*. Quest Publishing: Rock Island, Illinois.

Folmar, J.K. Editor. (1986). *"This State of Wonders" The Letters of an Iowa Frontier Family 1858-1861*. University of Iowa Press: Iowa City.

McCutcheon, M. (1993). *The Writer's Guide to Everyday Life in the 1800s*. Writer's Digest Books: Cincinnati, Ohio.

Morain, T., Nielson, L. & Schwieder, D. (2011). *Iowa Past to Present: The People and the Prairie, Revised Third Edition (Iowa and the Midwest Experience)*. University of Iowa Press: Iowa City.

Sage, L. (1987). *A History of Iowa (Iowa Heritage Collection)*. Iowa State Press.

Tjernagel, N. (2009). *The Passing of the Prairie by a Fossil: Biographical Sketches of Central Iowa Pioneers and Civil War Veterans*. AuthorHouse: Bloomington, Indiana.

Wolfe, P. (1911). *Wolfe's history of Clinton County, Iowa Volume 1*.

Wolfe, P. (1911). *Wolfe's history of Clinton County, Iowa Volume 2.*

ABOUT THE AUTHOR

Jodie Toohey is the author of three other novels – *Missing Emily: Croatian Life Letters*, *Melody Madson – May It Please the Court?*, and *Taming the Twisted* – as well as three poetry collections – *Crush and Other Love Poems for Girls*, *The Other Side of Crazy*, and *Versed in Nature: Hiking Northwest Illinois and East Iowa State Parks*. Her next novel's story will take place sometime between 1890 and 1910 when families camped along the Mississippi River in Camanche, Iowa, to harvest claims for button factories.

When Jodie is not writing poetry or fiction, she is helping authors, soon-to-be-authors, and want-to-be authors from pre-idea to reader through her company, Wordsy Woman Author Services. She lives in Iowa with her husband, daughter, son, and beagle, Maizey.

Learn more about Jodie's books, download bonuses, and sign up to receive updates at jodietoohey.com.
Learn more about her authors' services at wordsywomanforauthors.com.

If you enjoyed this book, please consider leaving a four- or five-star review on Amazon, Barnes & Noble, Goodreads, or elsewhere.
Thank you!